THE HODGKISS MYSTERIES

Hodgkiss and the Moving Body

Hodgkiss and the Death at the Wicket

Hodgkiss and the Poison Pen

PETER SINCLAIR

About the author

Peter Sinclair has spent most of his working life writing. He began reporting courts and councils in rural Orange (NSW) in the late 1950s then worked briefly for *The Sydney Daily Telegraph* where, because of his fluent shorthand, he was sentenced first to report local councils then banished to the Coroner's Court.

He'd had enough of sudden death and murder when opportunity knocked and he joined the staff of a new, large weekly paper in Sydney's northern suburbs, *The North Shore Times* where he was soon reporting councils again.

In 1965, he climbed over the journalistic fence to work as press secretary for a succession of NSW cabinet ministers (both Liberal and Labor) until 1991. Since then, he has made guest reappearances to help out in the PR sections of government departments.

His absorbing hobby is playing the piano. He has made a number of CDs in very limited editions. The titles tell it all: Peter Murders Mozart, Wrecks Rachmaninoff and Desecrates Debussy. He says he gives them away to people he doesn't like!

He has been married to Margaret for fifty-seven years and they have two sons; Sam, who is married to Carolyn with one son, Harry, 18, and Patrick who is married to Beejai with twin boys, Jackson and Zachary, aged 13.

Published in Australia by Peter Sinclair

First published in Australia 2020
Copyright © Peter Sinclair 2020
Cover design, typesetting: WorkingType Studio

The right of Peter Sinclair to be identified as the Author of the Work has been asserted in accordance with the Copyright, Designs and Patents Act 1988.

The Hodgkiss Mysteries Volume XIII
ISBN: 978-0-6489252-8-6
Sinclair, Peter
pp180

For Margaret

Author's Note

It has been no easy task to assemble material in order to reconstruct these accounts of the extraordinary contributions which Edgar Hodgkiss made to criminal detection over the years in which he was active in the field.

Hodgkiss himself kept no records.

When he suggested solutions to investigations being undertaken by his son-in-law, Detective Sergeant Donald Burke, Hodgkiss was convinced that he was merely stating the obvious and that his contributions were unremarkable and not worthy of record.

However, this presumption that he was 'merely stating the obvious' was frequently the cause of acrimony between himself and Sergeant Burke who resented the implied slur on his own powers of observation.

Fortunately for readers of these reports (and for posterity), Hodgkiss's daughter, Esme, kept detailed records in a series of exercise books which she has kindly made available to those of us interested in researching and recording the contributions made by this unique character.

Jan Campbell-Jones, the General Manager of Kanundda Council during this testing period of its history, also kindly consented to assist by releasing relevant documents from her personal files and from council's own official records system.

Ms Campbell-Jones also graciously agreed to be interviewed and has given accounts of many of these extraordinary events from her point of view, relying on her remarkable powers of recall to provide in some cases verbatim accounts of significant conversations. In addition she has allowed us access to the many emails that passed between Hodgkiss and herself. Hodgkiss, of course, had deleted these emails from his laptop within days, or in some instances, within hours of transmission.

I am indebted also to the many members of community organisations who supported Edgar Hodgkiss in his various campaigns against what he saw as the deficiencies of Kanundda Council and who have helped me verify many important details.

Readers of these records should note that they do not appear in chronological order therefore minor temporal inconsistencies may appear.

Many incidents in which Hodgkiss played an important role have not yet been committed to paper and many others, unfortunately, will never appear on the public record.

On occasions both the innocent and the guilty must be protected.

Peter Sinclair,
Lillimoor, 2011

Hodgkiss and the Moving Body

Even in death Katie Pye looked good.

But Evan White was no longer in the mood to enjoy the sight.

The girl was becoming a problem.

Moments earlier he had been standing beside the bed removing his briefs when he heard Katie make a soft grunting sound followed by a hiccup then a sigh.

He had turned to see the her lying there, naked, on top of the sheets, eyes closed, a slight smile curving her full lips.

He thought, Gawd, she's gone back to sleep.

'Time to get dressed,' he said briskly as he turned and headed for the ensuite.

At the door he glanced back to see if the hint had been taken.

But Katie had not moved.

'Katie! Time's getting on,' he said, an edge of anger in his voice now. 'I've got an early start today.'

Still no response from the girl.

'Katie. Please. Get dressed. I'm going for a shower now. OK?'

When the girl still lay motionless Evan felt the first tingle of fear.

He hurried to the bedside and leaned down. He said her name. Again … louder. Still no response.

He placed a hand on her shoulder and shook her gently.

Then he placed two fingers against the right side of the neck in the manner prescribed by the directors of TV crime dramas.

Nothing.

He scooped up the mobile phone from the bedside table and jabbed the keypad urgently.

'Bob. Get hold of Frank and get over here now. Yes. I know what the time is. Just get over here. It's urgent. It's Katie. I think she's dead.'

A voice, a man's, crackled through the tiny phone. 'Dead. She can't be. Are you sure?'

'I'm pretty sure,' said Evan. 'Just get Frank and get here quick … real quick.'

When his party won government at the recent elections Evan White had been appointed Minister for Local Government.

Upon arrival at his office on day one of the new government, Evan had been greeted deferentially by the permanent head of the department, a short jolly man with a florid face and a nose criss-crossed with veins. The permanent head had presented him with a slim folder containing documents which set out his duties and responsibilities as minister and at the rear of the folder a sheet setting out his entitlement to a personal staff of fifteen people at handsome rates of pay. These positions, Evan had already allocated almost exclusively to party faithful from the branches that had selected and served him during the campaign.

Among these fortunate appointees was Katie Pye, who had recently become his mistress. Now she also filled the position ' of assistant private secretary.

At the bottom of the list was two positions of Service Officer whose duties were defined as; 'To assist the Minister as required.'

These positions were now filled by Frank Appleby and Bob Roberts, two long term party members, known more for their loyalty than nous and discretion.

Upon hearing of these appointments one of his branch presidents had rung him. 'D'you think Katie's a good idea. I mean no doubt she's a good little goer between the sheets, mate, and good luck to you. But she's known for popping pills too, isn't she? But it's up to you of course. But Frank and Bob. I mean, well, they're not what you'd call the sharpest tools in the shed.'

Evan had agreed. 'But they've stuck by me through thick and thin so I've gotta stick by them. Besides, they're good men to have with you in a tight spot.'

'Well, don't get into too many tight spots, mate,' the branch president had warned him, then rung off.

Evan shook his head. The present situation certainly qualified as a tight spot.

He replaced the phone on the beside table then pulled up the sheet over the naked body.

Evan was in no doubt what had killed the girl. It must have been the pills she popped just before that last vigourous bout of love-making.

One thing was certain. Her body must not be found in his bedroom.

He hurried to the window and looked out into the dark street.

Katie's small red sports car was where she always left it; under the street light directly opposite. He had told her many times to turn into the driveway and park out of sight behind his house, but she had refused, saying she wouldn't be able to reverse out into the street in the dark. 'It's hard enough backing out in broad daylight let alone in the middle of the night,' she had told him.

And he had not volunteered to back the car out for her at night on those occasions when she did not stay over, since this would involve getting dressed again.

He returned to the bed, stripped off his briefs and went to the ensuite to shower.

He had just finished toweling himself dry when the front door chimes sounded.

He pulled on a dressing gown and hurried down the long central hall.

'Come in,' he said, pulling the door back.

Bob Roberts and Frank Appleby stood on the doorstep. Both looked worried.

'What's happened, boss?' Frank asked.

'She died,' said Evan. 'That's all I can tell you. It's all I know.'

He turned and walked back to the bedroom, the other two following.

When they reached the bedroom the two men stopped at the door, their eyes on the bed where the thin sheet did little to conceal what lay beneath.

'Have you called a doctor?'

'No, Frank I have *not* called a doctor. I called you and Bob. You understand that she can't be found here. You *do* understand that?'

Both men nodded lugubriously.

Both knew what would be the consequences if it became known that the assistant private secretary to the Minister for Local Government was found dead in her boss's bed.

They both knew, too, that if the Premier decided that Evan was a liability too big to carry when the news came out, they, along with their minister, would be out of a well-paid job.

And they knew from experience that it was up to them, as ministerial gophers, to once again pick up the messy pieces after one of their master's indulgences.

Both had warned him that this girl, with her well-known drug preferences and extremely liberal attitude towards sex, was a walking time bomb.

Frank asked wearily. 'So what do you want us to do?'

'I want you to take her home.'

'Take her home?' Bob echoed. 'I suppose you know where she lives.'

'Of course I know where she lives. I'll give you the address. It's a town house in Rosbury, not far from here. The keys'll be in her handbag there.'

He indicated a small black clutch bag on a chair near the door to the ensuite.

'Her car keys'll be there too I suppose.'

'You want us to take her car?'

'Well I certainly don't want it left standing outside until the police come for it. They might make a connection with this place. I suggest one of you drive her home in her car and the other follow in your car. Her town house has got a built-in garage so you should be able to take her straight inside without anyone seeing you.'

'But what about taking her out to her car. We can't just carry her across the street like that … under a sheet.'

'I'm not suggesting you should. We'll slip her into one of my overcoats and the two of you can take her out between you, supporting her as if she'd had too much to drink. God knows I've had to do that on my own often enough in the past.'

He crossed to a built-in wardrobe and took out a dark overcoat. 'Here,' he said, tossing it to Frank. 'Get her into that.'

Frank caught the garment and Evan went to the bed and pulled back the sheet.

Both men glanced then quickly looked away.

Ignoring their embarrassment, Evan said. 'Here, Bob, lend me a hand.'

Gingerly, and taking elaborate care not to touch the girl in a disrespectful or intimate way, Bob and Frank assisted Evan to raise the naked girl from the bed and with considerable difficultly the three men manoeuvred her into the overcoat.

'There, job done,' said Evan. 'Now just walk her over the road between you, get her into the car and take her home. Ring me when it's done, OK?'

He reached into the girl's handbag and took out a key ring with a bunch of keys attached.

He tossed them to Frank. 'I expect the car keys and the keys to her town house will be on this, but have a look around first because she lives with a girlfriend.'

'Oh great,' said Frank. 'And what do we do if the girlfriend's at home.'

Evan waved an arm. 'Use your initiative. Take her home … anywhere. Just don't bring her back here. If you run into a problem give me a bell.'

After they had left, supporting the girl awkwardly between them, Evan hurried to a front window.

He watched anxiously as the odd trio staggered down the pathway from the front door towards the street.

In his clumsy attempt to lower her into the passenger's seat of the tiny car Frank lost his grasp on the girl and she fell against the nearside mudguard then onto the roadway. Her arm struck the ground heavily.

'Hey, careful with her,' said Bob

'Don't worry. She's not feeling a thing,' said Frank.

They both sniggered.

At last the car drove away, Frank at the wheel, Bob followed in his own car.

* * *

Phyllis Thomson, now in her sixtieth year, had been troubled with insomnia since the death of her husband three years ago.

Frequently, rather than lay awake by the hour, she rose, put on her dressing gown and prowled the grounds of the rather down-at-heels blocks of flats where she and her husband had passed the thirty-two years of their married life.

Sometimes she would pull on a skirt and walk the streets until she felt weary enough to court sleep once more.

This particular night was no different to many others. She woke about midnight, tried to compose herself to sleep again, but knowing that sleep would not come she had swung her feet over the side of the bed, pulled on her ancient slippers and gone out to the kitchen. She would make a cup of cocoa and put on the television. Perhaps she would go to sleep in front of the tele. That had happened many times before and she had woken up with the dawn, cramped and dry-mouthed.

In her kitchen Phyllis lost no time in heating some milk in a saucepan and mixing in the cocoa powder and sugar. When it was heated to a comfortable drinkable temperature, she poured it into a mug and since it was a warm night, she decided to take the drink to the tiny balcony off the kitchen and sit there to enjoy it. From the balcony Phyllis had a good view of the road outside.

That little red sports car was parked there again, which meant the woman, no, not a woman, she was really little more than a girl, would be visiting the man who lived in the rather grand house opposite.

Of course Phyllis knew who it was who lived there. Everyone in her block knew about him. Everyone in the street, probably. The important politician. A minister in the government.

Then something on the verandah of the house opposite caught her eye.

The front door had opened and in the light from the hall inside Phyllis witnessed a rather remarkable sight. Three people, in a huddled group stood on the verandah then began an awkward, precarious progress down the front path towards the roadway.

The two on either side she saw were men and they appeared to be supporting the person in the middle who was wearing an overcoat.

The three reached the kerb and continued, in a weaving, unsteady manner across the road towards the little car parked outside her flats.

When the huddled, struggling group reached the car one of the men detached and hurried around the car to open the door on the passenger's side.

Almost at once the other man, who had been left alone to support the third person, lost his grip and person in the overcoat fell heavily against the car then onto the roadway.

She heard a muttered exchange between the men followed by a snigger.

As the figure lay on the ground Phyllis saw that the overcoat had fallen open and she was in no doubt that the wearer was a young woman who had nothing on under it.

At once she came to her feet and uttered an involuntary cry in sympathy with the girl who now was lying on her back, unmoving on the roadway.

Both men immediately looked up towards the balcony, scowling, guilt written on their faces.

She snorted her contempt. Of course she already knew the sort of things that went on over the road at that fellow's house. Naked girls and these rough sort of men.

There had been frequent loud parties in the past. When she had rung the house to complain she had been ignored. On one occasion the man who answered her appeal for quiet had abused her in the most foul language.

She had rung the police on that occasion and on several subsequent occasions when noise exceeded what she regarded as a reasonable level, but the police had told her they could do nothing about it.

That minister fellow who lived over the road should be ashamed of himself having young girls like that in and out of his house and so drunk they couldn't stand up on their own two feet without being carried.

She decided, not for the first time, to ring the police and report what she regarded as improper goings-on in her neighbourhood.

*   *   *

Evan had settled in front of the huge television in his living room when the mobile beside him rang.

He glanced at the screen. It was Frank, no doubt ringing to report.

'Yes, Frank. So how'd it go? Did you get her inside all right?"

'Went fine, boss. No sweat,' he said. 'The keys to her place were on the ring like you said. The girlfriend was out and we got in OK.'

'So where did you leave her?'

'We sat her up in the lounge and put the TV on.'

Evan sat bolt upright. 'You sat her up in the lounge in front of the TV … in the nude?'

'Oh no. We dressed her first.'

Evan's mouth fell open. 'You dressed her! What did you dress her in? Her clothes are still here.'

'We know that,' Frank said in the tone of one explaining the obvious to a backward child. 'But it was no problem. There were tons of clothes there at her place. Wardrobes full of them. Between them those two sheilas had more clothes than they could have worn in two lifetimes. We reckoned it just didn't seem right to leave her sitting there with nothin' on.'

'OK, OK. We'll leave it at that then,' said Evan.

He cut the call, staring blankly at the TV.

*   *   *

'Oh put a sock in it you two. I've been listening to the pair of you going over and over this business and getting nowhere. And it's all a lot of nonsense, what you've been saying.'

Esme Burke was quite out of patience.

Her husband, Detective Inspector Donald Burke, and her father, Edgar Hodgkiss, were eyeing each other aggressively across the narrow table in the built-in pine breakfast nook in the kitchen of the Burke's home in a back street of suburban Lillimoor.

'It's not nonsense,' Hodgkiss objected. 'Donald just won't admit that in order to be an effective investigator ...'

'And who says Donald *isn't* an effective investigator,' Esme demanded.

'My dear,' said Hodgkiss sweetly. 'You have only to look at the facts ... look at his record of performance.'

'Yes, look at it,' said Esme. 'How many times has Superintendent O'Hare commended him for ...'

Hodgkiss held up a hand. 'Please, Esme. Let us not go into that. You know as well as I that ...'

But his daughter cut him off. 'Yes, Dad I know what you're going to say and I'm absolutely astonished that you'd think of throwing something like that up at us after all this time.'

Hodgkiss protested. 'But surely in the context of what we were discussing it's only fair to point out that if it had not been for my input into many of Donald's most high profile investigations, he would never ...'

Donald decided to enter the fray. 'But aren't we getting off the point. I've never said that you haven't helped on occasions, Dad. You have. We both admit that. What I won't agree to is that I wouldn't have eventually got there under my own steam. A well-conducted police investigation follows certain procedures and we always get there in the end ... or nearly always.'

'Yes,' Hodgkiss interjected. 'Certain procedures. That's your problem. That's why police officers are sometimes referred to as Constable Plods ... because they plod along, following their petty procedures when many times, as I've demonstrated, you can solve your cases much quicker with the use of a little imagination ... a little bit of lateral thinking ... thinking outside the square.'

And so the argument progressed through peaks of outrage and troughs of conciliation until at last Esme negotiated a truce which included a clause binding them to meet at noon the following day for a counter lunch at a hotel near the Crestwood police station where Donald worked.

Consequently, the following day Hodgkiss was sitting in the reception area of the Crestwood patrol shortly before noon.

He had explained to the corpulent sergeant behind the long counter that he was waiting for Inspector Burke and the sergeant had rung through to inform Donald of his arrival.

'He said he won't be a moment,' the sergeant had confided and Hodgkiss had settled back in an uncomfortable chrome chair to await Donald's pleasure.

Then a phone rang.

On the other side of the counter the sergeant picked up the receiver.

'Crestwood Patrol. Sergeant Anderson speaking.'

A lengthy pause. 'One moment madam. Your name please. Yes. Without a P. Go on. (pause). Yes, I know the building. On the corner of Kryten Street isn't it. Old three storey block. Right? And how do you know they were drunk? You think one of them was a woman. If she had an overcoat on you must have x-ray vision. (Pause). I see. Very well. And can you say what make it was. Small, was it? Yes, I agree they do all tend to look the same. And the colour. You're sure. Red. It can be tricky at night. Very well then. Yes. I'll make a report. Yes. I'll let him know. No, I can't promise that. Thank you.'

Hodgkiss heard the receiver put down heavily then the muttered words 'bloody old pest.'

Hodgkiss was about to stand and issue a reprimand to the sergeant when Donald appeared through a door in the wall opposite where Hodgkiss sat.

Hodgkiss glanced at his watched and rose as Donald approached. 'You're late.'

'Nonsense, Dad. I'm right on time,' said Donald, unabashed.

As they walked down the front steps of the building a tabletop truck turned into the forecourt with a small red sports car on its tray.

'A new toy for the highway patrol, is it?' Hodgkiss asked with a nod towards the vehicle.

Donald shook his head. 'Nah. It's here for forensic testing.'

'One of your cases, is it?' Hodgkiss asked with a poor attempt at concealing his interest.

'Yeah. But nothing for you to get excited about. Not a murder. Nothing juicy for you to exercise your great lateral thinking on.'

'What then?'

'Just another bimbo who overdosed. Good riddance I say. Better off out of the gene pool.'

Nevertheless Hodgkiss was careful to memorize the number of the car as it disappeared around a corner of the building to a holding yard at the rear.

When they were settled at the bar, their beers in front of them and their lunches ordered, Hodgkiss asked: 'And what do you expect to find in the car?'

Donald looked up in surprise. 'Find in what car?'

'The little sports car they were taking into the station as we came out. What do you hope to learn from the forensic examination?'

Donald shook his head. 'Not a lot. Probably nothing. I told you, Dad. It's a straight forward OD. Another druggie bites the dust.'

'No doubt, Donald, but how many times have I heard you say one of your cases is straight forward and it's turned out to be nothing of the sort?'

'Well, this time, Dad, you can take it as gospel. No risk.'

'So where was she found?'

'She lives … lived in a town house in Rosbury. The girl she shared with came home and found her sitting up in front of the tele … dead.'

'An overdose, you say. Had she come to the notice of the police as a drug user.'

Donald shrugged. 'Nothing known, but that doesn't mean that she hadn't been using the stuff for years. Her girl friend said she did, although we didn't find any stuff in her room.'

'I suppose she must have had a regular job in order to support this habit.'

'Yes, she had a regular job although I don't know how well it paid?'

'So what did she do?'

'Public servant … or that's what her friend told us.'

'And was it true? Was she a public servant?'

'Yes, I suppose you could say she was. She worked for one of the minister's in the State Government.'

Hodgkiss interest sparked up. 'Did she indeed? Which minister?'

Donald could not contain his irritation. 'Hell, Dad. I don't know which minister. Does it matter?'

Hodgkiss shook his head. 'Donald. At this stage we have no idea what matters and what doesn't.'

Donald's jaw dropped. 'Am I hearing right? Did you say "we"? Now, Dad, please don't tell me that you seriously think there's something suspicious about this girl's death?'

Hodgkiss shrugged, but said nothing.

'OK. You go ahead and make a fool of yourself,' said Donald. 'Because if you go charging in, like you usually do, thinking you're going to uncover some dastardly crime, let me tell you that you're going to finish up looking a complete fool.'

Again Hodgkiss shrugged. 'Perhaps ... perhaps not. We'll see. I seem to recall that you've told me that before and it was not I that looked like a complete fool in the end.'

*   *   *

Esme was sitting in the family room reading the local paper, The *Northern Star,* when Hodgkiss found her.

'Esme, do you know how to find Kryten Street in Rosbury?'

Esme lowered the paper onto her lap. 'Never heard of it. Why do you ask?'

'I need to go there this morning.'

Esme looked up suspiciously. 'Do you? And who do you know that lives in Kryten Street?'

'There's a lady there I need to speak to.'

'And what do you need to speak to this lady about?'

'Esme, it's a long and rather involved story. You do not need to know the details and I promise you that my visit will not be a long one. I will not hold you up for more than ten minutes.'

'Dad, this isn't to do with one of Donald's investigations, is it? You know how he feels about you interfering.'

'How would I know if it's to do with one of his investigations? I don't know of *any* investigation he's involved with at the moment. He hasn't bothered to tell me. And as for interfering, can you honestly say that I have interfered with Donald's career as a police officer. Wouldn't it be fair to say that my occasional involvement in his investigations has been wholly beneficial?'

'I wouldn't argue with that for one moment, Dad. But you know how he feels about it.'

'Yes, Esme, I know exactly how Donald feels about it. But the question is what do *you* feel about it, and do you intend to take me to this address or must I resort to alternate means of travel?'

This reference to 'alternate means of travel' was a well-tried-and-tested threat to ring for a cab, a tactic which invariably brought Esme to terms. 'No one's going to pay for a taxi while there's a perfectly good car in our garage,' was the invariable response to what Hodgkiss thought of as his Taxi Gambit.

'No need to call a cab, Dad,' said Esme putting down the newspaper and getting up. "I suppose you know where this Kryten Street is?'

'Yes. I've checked it on the street map.'

'Come on then. Let's get going. I can do some shopping at the Lillimoor Village on the way home.'

Ten minutes later Esme was parking the small beige sedan outside a rather down-at-heels three storey block of flats on a corner.

'Is this the place?' she asked as Hodgkiss climbed from the car onto the overgrown nature strip.

'I think so. The place I need is in Kryten Street on a corner. This is the only block of flats on a corner in the street so far as I can see.'

'So which flat does this person live in?'

'That's what I've yet to work out,' said Hodgkiss heading for a wrought iron gate in the low brick wall.

'You mean you don't even know the name of the person you're looking for?' Esme called after him.

'Something like that,' Hodgkiss muttered inaudibly as he headed down the path to the entry porch.

Just inside the front door was a list of occupants.

'That will be her,' Hodgkiss said to himself, smiling, nodding and dabbing a finger at one of the names on the list ... Mrs P. Thomson, flat 2.

'Thompson without a P.' Hodgkiss nodded and headed for a door with a brass 2 attached on the other side of the entry hall.

He was about to wield the brass knocker in the form of a fist when the door opened and a woman, whose age Hodgkiss estimated to be in the early sixties, stood in the doorway.

'Mrs Thomson?' Hodgkiss inquired politely.

'Yes, that's me,' said the woman.' How can I help you? I was just on my way out.'

'I won't keep you a moment,' said Hodgkiss. 'I just wanted to speak to you about the call you made to the police station yesterday morning in connection with what you saw outside last night.'

'Early morning it was,' said Mrs Thomson. 'After midnight it would have been.' She looked him up and down. 'Are you from the police? You don't look like a policeman to me.'

'I'm not actually a policeman of course,' Hodgkiss confessed with an ingratiating smile, 'but my son-in-law, Inspector Burke, is investigating the matter and I'm trying to help him with some of the legwork. They're very pressed, our police, and they need all the help they can get.'

Mrs Thomson smiled. 'Very well then Mr ...?

'Hodgkiss. Edgar Hodgkiss. Now would you tell me what you saw exactly?'

'Well, I couldn't sleep so I'd gone out to the kitchen to make myself a cup of cocoa. I went out on the balcony for a bit of air and saw what looked like three people come out of the house opposite. They were in a sort of a huddle and I thought at first that they were probably a little the worse for wear. You know ... under the weather.'

'Drunk, you mean, Hodgkiss provided.

'Yes, drunk. I thought at first it was three fellows but when one of them was trying to put one of the others in the car ...'

'What car was that, Mrs Thomson?' Hodgkiss asked.

'It was the girl's car. A little red sports car. She often leaves it parked right outside under the street light. The two men were supporting the girl back to her car. Almost carrying her. But when they got her there one of them went around to the other side of the car to open the door and it was then that the other fellow, who was trying to hold her up on his own, he dropped her. It was then that I noticed that she was a woman.'

'Why was that?'

'Well, when the fellow dropped her on the road the overcoat she was wearing fell open and she had nothing on underneath. Anyone could have seen that it wasn't a man lying there.'

Hodgkiss nodded. 'I see. So what happened then?'

'The two of them bundled her into the car; one of them got in and drove off and the other fellow went off after them in another car that had been parked a bit further down the road.'

'And what can you tell me about this second car that followed the one with the girl in?'

'Not a lot. I didn't really take much notice. It was much bigger than the girl's little red car.'

'Did you notice if it was a sedan, a station wagon an SUV ...?

'Just an ordinary car. A sedan I suppose. Dark.'

Hodgkiss nodded. Thank you, Mrs Thomson. Now, you're sure, are you, that these three people came from the house opposite.'

'Oh yes. I know that because that girl often goes there. She's in and out of there all the time.'

'And these two men; had you ever seen them before?'

Mrs Thomson frowned and shook her head. 'Yes, I'm pretty sure I have, but there's always people coming and going there.'

'And do you know who lives there?'

'Oh yes, I know all about him. He's one of those political fellows in the government. All I can say is that I don't think very much of him and his friends. They've got absolutely no regard for the neighbours with all the noisy wild parties that go on there. And of course that girl's always there.'

Hodgkiss decided that he had learned about as much as he could from Mrs Thomson.

'If you're going out perhaps my daughter could give you a lift somewhere. We're going to the shops at Lillimoor. Would that be any help?'

'That would be very handy. Save me waiting for the bus. They're always running late. Can you wait a moment? I just need to grab a bag from the kitchen. Now you're quite sure, are you, that your daughter won't mind dropping me off.'

And so Hodgkiss made the introductions when they returned to the car and Esme agreed, smiling, to drive Mrs Thomson to the village shops at Lillimoor.

As Hodgkiss and Mrs Thomson were about to climb into Esme's car a large dark sedan turned into the driveway of the house opposite.

Hodgkiss noticed that the car slowed almost to a stop beside them and the occupants of the car, two men, looked hard at him and Mrs Thomson as he opened the rear door for her to take the back seat.

'That looks like the car I saw last night,' Mrs Thomson said, pointing. 'The one that followed the little red car with the girl in it. I couldn't be certain, but I suppose they could have been the fellows who carried her out and drove off with her.'

Hodgkiss nodded. It seemed quite likely, he thought.

And it also seemed to Hodgkiss that the occupants of the other car had taken more than a passing interest in Mrs Thomson and himself.

Esme, too, had not missed the two angry, scowling faces and she felt distinctly uneasy.

'Dad, who were those two men in the car that just turned into the big house opposite. I didn't at all like the way they looked at you. What's been going on?'

But before Hodgkiss could think of a suitably comforting response Mrs Thomson had her say. 'Those are the two fellows who I saw last night, or rather this morning, carrying some poor girl out of that place where those fellows were turning in just now. I was out on my balcony and I saw one of them drop the poor girl on the road and unfortunately they just happened to look up and saw me watching them. I think they might have thought I was spying on them or something like that. But I wasn't really. I was just having a cup of cocoa because I couldn't get off to sleep.'

Esme sent an anxious glance towards her father as she put the car into gear and headed for the Lillimoor shopping village.

After dropping Mrs Thomson near the Lillimoor railway station Esme drove into the large parking area at the rear of the shops and climbed out of the car. 'I won't be long, Dad,' she said and set off.

Hodgkiss spent half an hour browsing in a local charity shop and when he returned to the car Esme was waiting for him.

'Donald rang,' she said. 'He's at home. Came home for morning tea. He'll have to be told.'

Hodgkiss blustered. 'Told about what? There's nothing to tell him.'

Esme shook her head. 'He'll have to be told about what Mrs Thomson said about the girl and the red car.'

'But that's got nothing to do with Donald.'

'I'm not sure about that. I know Donald is investigating something to do with a dead girl and a red car. He told me. He's having it tested by the forensic people now.'

Hodgkiss shook his head. 'Esme, how many red cars do you think there are on the North Side? If you tell Donald he'll just make a huge fuss over nothing.'

Esme started the car. 'He'll have to be told, Dad, and that's the end of it.'

Hodgkiss nodded. 'Very well. Be it on your head.'

He began mentally preparing his defence.

*   *   *

Evan White was at his study window when he saw the sedan turn in slowly and disappear down the driveway to the rear of the house.

He hurried through to the kitchen.

Now to find out just how badly those two morons stuffed things up last night.

He opened the back door just in time to see Frank and Bob, heads together on the back deck, whispering.

Getting their story straight, he thought.

'Come in boys,' he said with an attempt at camaraderie. 'Cuppa?'

Soon the three were settled around the kitchen table. Evan closed the red suitcase containing the departmental files he had been working on earlier in the day, and placed it on the floor.

'You actually dressed her, right? I won't ask why. What I'd like to know is what did you do with my overcoat ... the one she was wearing when you left with her?'

Frank and Bob looked at each other, open mouthed.

Frank started to say something, then stopped.

'You're not going to tell me you left it at her place, are you?'

After a short silence Frank said: 'You're not worrying about it, are you, boss? I mean it didn't have your name in it or anything like that, did it?'

'No. It didn't have my name in it. I don't put my name on my clothes … not since I was at boarding school.'

Obviously his assistants' general knowledge did not extend to DNA.

Frank said: 'Thing is we were in a bit of a hurry. We heard someone arriving and got out quick smart.'

'And who was arriving?'

'Some girl,' said Bob. 'We didn't get a good look at her because we'd gone out the back way and she'd come in the front.'

Evan nodded. 'It was probably the girl she shares with. She must've reported it to the police because it was over the news at six.'

'What did they say exactly?' Bob asked.

'Just that a girl was found dead … suspected overdose … nothing more,' said Evan. 'Didn't give her name.'

He paused then continued. 'Just one more thing, boys. These clothes you put on her. How do you know they were hers? They could have belonged to this other girl that she shared with.'

Bob and Frank shrugged in unison.

Bob said. 'Probably were hers. They certainly fitted her OK.'

Evan winced and pushed back his chair. 'OK, Now remember; you two were here all evening until at least two in the morning. Right?'

Again an anxious glance passed between the two men.

'So what's the matter now?' Evan asked.

'It's nothing much, but you know the old bitch over the road who's always banging on about your parties being too noisy?'

Evan nodded. 'Mrs Thomson. Yes. What about her?'

'Well, she was out on her balcony last night, in the middle of the night would you believe, and she saw us carrying Katie out to the car and driving off.'

Evan nodded. 'So?'

'Well, Frank dropped her.'

Frank cut in indignantly. 'I couldn't help it. She's heavier than she looks and Bob had gone around to open the door on the other side so we could put in her. I just lost my grip on her.'

Evan clenched his teeth. 'OK. Anything else I need to know?'

'Just one more thing,' said Bob, 'although it's probably not important.'

Evan sighed. 'And what is this one more thing that's probably not important?'

'When we arrived just now I saw that lady Mrs Thomson from over the road talking to an old guy outside in the street. They got into a car parked outside the flats. And the old guy, I've got a feeling I've seen him before somewhere, but I can't remember where.'

'Is that all?' Evan asked through clenched teeth.

'Yeah. That's about it. Oh yeah, and Frank made a note of the number of this car she got in just in case.'

'Well, let's hope that nothing more comes of it … the whole business,' Evan said, although he had a sick sinking feeling as he reviewed the catastrophe that the evening had become.

But if the worst came to the worst his cabinet colleague, the Minister for Police and Justice, owed him some serious favours for services rendered.

He might have to call in a few if the brown stuff really hit the fan over this business.

When the two men had left Evan sat at his desk and reached for one of the red boxes containing his ministerial papers. He had been at work for less than ten minutes when he reached for the silver box containing his cigarettes. He took out a cigarette and placed it between his lips. Then he reached into his slacks pocket for the silver lighter presented to him by a grateful branch member for whom he had found a lucrative post in the party's head office.

The lighter wasn't in the pocket. He patted the other pocket but the lighter wasn't there either.

He stood up and looked around.

Then with a frisson of horror he remembered.

The overcoat.

He reached for his mobile phone.

'Frank. That overcoat of mine you and Bob left behind at the girl's place. I need it back … now. It's urgent.'

There was a short pause while Bob mulled over this instruction. 'OK, boss. Frank and I will run over there now and see what we can do.'

'No, Bob. You won't run over and see what you can do. You will run over and GET THAT OVERCOAT.'

'OK boss. But what if there's no one at home. I think the girl she lived with goes out to work.'

'All the better. Just get in, get the coat and get back here, Right? Pronto.'

'Yeah. Right boss.'.

*　　*　　*

Donald had parked his unmarked police car at the kerb, leaving the driveway clear for Esme to park in the garage.

Hodgkiss helped her carry the shopping in through the laundry to the kitchen where Donald was sitting in the breakfast nook, a mug of instant coffee in front of him.

A cream biscuit was halfway to his mouth.

'Back at last,' he remarked. 'I suppose you've bought up half of Lillimoor.'

'No, Donald,' said Esme, 'just enough to keep the supply of food up to you for the next day or two.'

She began to unload the shopping from the bags onto the bench.

Without looking up she said. 'Dad's got something to tell you, Donald.'

'Oh has he?' said Donald, turning to Hodgkiss who had slid into the other side of the breakfast nook. 'OK Dad. What's it about?'

'It's nothing, Donald. Esme has got some idea into her head and I haven't the least notion what …'

Esme cut him off. 'Dad. Are you going to tell him or am I?'

Now Donald was starting to worry.

'You haven't been interfering again have you?' He glared across the table. Louder. 'Have you?'

'No, of course not. Esme has run away with the idea that something I'm following up might have some bearing on an investigation of yours. But since I have no idea what cases you're on at present I don't see how I could possibly be interfering.'

'OK. Then, where were you this morning?' Donald asked, his suspicions now turned to anxiety.

'I just asked Esme to take me to visit a lady I wanted to talk to about a particularly private matter.'

'A lady you wanted to talk to, eh? What lady and where does she live.'

'It's no one you'd know Donald. I see no point in ...'

But Esme would cut her father no slack. 'Her name is Mrs Phyllis Thomson and she lives in a block of flats on a corner in Kryten Street.'

Donald's eye narrowed. Anxiety had turned into alarm. 'Kryten Street! And what the hell were you doing in Kryten Street, Dad?'

'Esme told you,' said Hodgkiss. 'I was visiting a lady ... a Mrs Thomson.'

Donald half-rose from the bench seat. 'Would this be the same Mrs Thomson who rang the station to complain about noise from a place opposite.'

'Really, Donald. I wouldn't know.'

'Then what *would* you know? Why did you want to talk to her?'

Hodgkiss drew himself up. 'Donald, that is my affair. It was a private conversation.'

Esme said quietly. 'Mrs Thomson said something about being on her balcony in the middle of the night and seeing two men carrying a girl out to a little red car parked outside her flats and dropping her on the road before driving away with her. That's right, isn't it, Dad?'

Donald exploded. 'You *have* been bloody interfering. Now, tell me, and no beating around the bush; who put you on to Mrs Thomson.' He held up a hand. 'No, wait just a minute. Don't tell me. I know. You were sitting in the reception area at the station eavesdropping when she rang. Right? Sergeant Anderson reckoned you'd been taking rather a lot of interest in what he was saying to her. Then on our way out to the pub you saw the red car brought in for testing. That's what happened, isn't it? That's how you knew?'

Hodgkiss decided that attack was the best defence.

'Yes, Donald. That's how I knew. I heard the sergeant ask for her name and then he said 'that's without a P,' or words to that effect. That's how I knew her name. Then he mentioned a block of flats on the corner of Kryten Street. It's a very short street. It was easy.'

'But why? Why bother to go and see her? Why take the trouble. It was just a complaint about noise or something. What was the point?'

Hodgkiss shook his head. 'You wouldn't understand, Donald.'

'Try me.'

'It would be a compete waste of time.'

'I'd like to know too, Dad,' said Esme. 'After all, you talked me into driving you there.'

'All right. I'll tell you both, but you won't like it, Donald. I decided to do something about it because of the shameful offhand way that sergeant treated the poor woman. I knew with one hundred percent certainty that he wasn't going to do anything about her problem … whatever it was.'

'And what made you think that?' Donald asked.

'After he'd finished the conversation he hung up and I heard him say quite distinctly: "Bloody old pest." Obviously he had no intention of doing anything to help.

'But Dad,' Donald protested, 'We get cranks ringing up all the time. We can't possibly follow up every little thing they whinge about.'

'I'm sure not everyone who rings up is a crank,' said Esme. 'The least you can do is to take them seriously, at first anyway.'

Seeing he had an ally Hodgkiss pressed the advantage home. 'Then there was *your* attitude.'

'*My* attitude,' said Donald defiantly. 'What was wrong with my attitude?'

'I don't suppose you'd remember what you said when we saw that red car being driven in.'

'No. Why should I?'

'You should remember because it demonstrated the same negative un-caring attitude as the sergeant.'

'OK. So what did I say?'

'You made light of the whole thing. When I asked about who owned the car you said words to the effect that it was just another bimbo who'd taken an overdose. Good riddance, you said. Better off out of the gene pool.'

Donald blushed and blustered. 'I didn't say that at all.'

'Donald, you did,' said Hodgkiss emphatically. 'I distinctly remember because I thought at the time how uncaring you were ... just like the sergeant.'

Donald appealed unconvincingly to Esme. 'I'm pretty sure I'd never have said anything like that.'

'Well, Dad's got a pretty good memory and if he says that's what you said I believe him. Besides, I can quite believe that's the sort of thing you *would* say. I've heard you say thoughtless things like that before.'

Deciding it was time to stop digging a deeper hole for himself, Donald changed tack. 'OK. Even if I did say something like that, and I don't agree that I did, it still give you an excuse to run off harassing that woman.'

'I didn't harass anyone, Donald, as I'm sure Esme will tell you.'

Esme considered for a moment. 'I only met the woman for a few minutes when I drove her to the station at Lillimoor but she didn't look to me as if she'd been harassed.'

'No, of course she didn't,' Hodgkiss confirmed.

Esme continued thoughtfully. 'But I must admit I was a bit concerned about those two fellows in the car that turned into the house opposite. They gave us a very dirty look and they slowed down as if they wanted to check on us.'

'What was that?' Donald demanded, sensing blood.

'It was nothing, Donald,' said Hodgkiss quickly. 'Esme's imagining things.'

'I'm doing nothing of the sort, Dad,' said Esme sharply. 'They *did* give us a dirty look. They gave you a dirty look in particular, and Mrs Thomson too. They seemed to know her.'

'And they turned into the big place opposite the flats?' Donald asked. 'Is that right?'

Esme nodded. 'Yes. Why? Do you know who lives there, Donald?'

'Yes, of course I know who lives there?'

'Who?' Esme asked.

'Never you mind. That's none of your business.'

Hodgkiss said. 'Don't talk nonsense, Donald. We could easily find out who lives there if you won't tell us. Mrs Thomson would know.'

Esme said. 'Now you mention it I remember Mrs Thomson saying the fellow who lived opposite was a politician.'

Hodgkiss nodded. 'You're right, Esme. She said he was "one of those political fellows", didn't she. And she didn't think much of him as I recall.' He turned to Esme. 'I suppose we should make him our next port of call.'

Donald snapped. 'You'll do nothing of the sort. There is a police investigation under way and you will not be helping if you continue to blunder about the landscape talking to people at random.'

Hodgkiss nodded. 'Very well, Donald. I concede that it may not be helpful if I was to continue my inquiry in that direction. However, I am interested to see where this girl lived … the one who took the overdose.'

'And why on earth would you want to go there?'

'Really, Donald. I've no idea. I won't know until I get there. It may prove to be a waste of time but that is what I intend to do next. So if you have the information on you perhaps you could give me the girl's address and save me the trouble.'

'No way, Dad. No way known.'

Hodgkiss shrugged. Very well, Donald. Then I will ascertain the address through my own resources.'

'And how will you do that.'

Hodgkiss smiled. 'I have my methods.'

*　　*　　*

Evan was waiting on the nature strip outside his home for the ministerial limousine to collect him when his mobile phone rang. He glanced at the caller's ID. He closed his eyes for a moment and inhaled deeply.

'Yes, Roger?' he asked.

Roger Carpenter was a developer with many projects planned and under way in various parts of Kanundda. Within the building industry Roger's projects were held in contempt for their cookie-cutter design and shoddy finish. There were also strong suspicions that Roger had on more than one occasion resorted to blackmail and bribery in order to secure council approvals.

'How's it going, mate,' Roger inquired. He did not need to elaborate. He had been waiting for advice from Evan that certain zoning problems, which the minister was uniquely placed to solve, had been settled in relation to a major subdivision in St James, regarded as one of the most desirable suburbs in Kanundda.

Roger had rung Evan several times in the past week without receiving the assurances of assistance he had hoped for.

'Nothing just yet, mate,' said Evan. 'But I've got the boys working on it.'

'When you say "the boys" we're talking about Bob and Frank. Right?'

'Yeah. Good men?'

'Do you think so? You know what I think? I think sometimes they get a little bit out of their depth. Sometimes I think you put them onto jobs they're not up to.'

Evan was not about to argue. 'Look, mate, if you're not happy I'll take an interest in this myself.'

'I thought you'd have taken an interest in it yourself before now seeing you've put your hand up for a couple of big ones. You're up to lose too if this doesn't go ahead soon. I can't keep the machinery on stand-by for ever you know. It costs big time.'

'Yeah, I realise that, mate. I'll have a talk to the planning people myself. They might take a bit more notice.'

'Let's bloody hope so,' said Roger, cutting the connection.

Bloody Frank. Bloody Bob.

Evan ground his teeth.

*   *   *

Next morning, after Donald, had left for work, Hodgkiss went to the privacy of the back deck, sat at one of the curved benches around the circular redwood table, took the mobile phone from his shirt pocket and thumbed the keypad.

In her office at the front of the Kanundda Council

Chambers building on the Northern Highway at Grattan, the general manager of the council, Jan Campbell-Jones, picked up her tiny blue phone.

She glanced at the caller's identification and opened the connection.

'Good morning Hodgkiss. Long time, no hear. Have you been away? Is all well in the Burke ménage?'

'All is as well as it can be when one is forced to live under the same roof as an intolerant son-in-law and ungrateful daughter.'

'Now now, Hodgkiss. You know that is most unfair. I understand about Donald, but I won't hear a bad word said against Esme. Anyway, what's the trouble now? Is it something I can help you with? I expect it must be or you wouldn't have rung. These days, Hodgkiss, you ring only when you want something. It is rather disappointing. But out with it. How may I help?

'Just a vehicle's number plate. I need to know the name and address of the owner.'

'I assume this relates to one of Donald's investigations, does it?'

'He seems to think so.'

'Then it's not a case where he has sought your input.'

'Far from it, I regret.'

'Oh dear. It's like that, is it?'

'I'm afraid so. Do you mind?'

'Not at all. Well, what's the number?'

Hodgkiss recited the number of the small red car he had seen being driven into the yard of the Crestwood police station.

'Can you manage that?' he asked.

'No trouble. I'll call you back shortly.'

Within an hour Jan rang back. 'The vehicle is registered to one Katie Pye and her address is 3/24 Arnold Street, Rosbury.'

'Thank you, Jan,' he said as he scribbled on a scrap of paper.

'Not at all. It's the least I can do considering all the help you've given me in the past.' After a short pause Jan continued. 'What do you know about Ms Pye?'

'Nothing whatsoever,' Hodgkiss replied, 'I take it from the inquiry that you know something about Ms Pye.'

'Indeed I do. I know that she works for one Evan White who happens to be the Minister for Local Government.'

Hodgkiss nodded. 'I was told she worked for a politician. So you've had contact with her in her professional capacity, have you?'

'No. Not with her but others from her minister's office have been in frequent contact with several of my councillors and some members of the planning staff.'

'Oh ho. Have they indeed. Putting pressure on for some shonky developer no doubt.'

'My my, Hodgkiss. What a cynic you've become.'

'And not without good reason. So Mr White is using his position to do favours for mates. Is that the picture?'

'That is the picture exactly and he is not going to get away with it. Now, this business Donald is involved in: is that likely to reflect poorly on the minister? Because if it is that would certainly help us resist any pressure from that quarter.'

'It's early days yet, Jan, but the way things are shaping up at the moment I'd say there is an excellent chance that the minister is very likely to finish up with a good deal of egg on his face.'

'Excellent. And will you kindly keep me informed.'

'You have my word.'

Hodgkiss cut the connection, folded the scrap of paper and placed it in his shirt pocket.

He pushed back the bench seat, rose and hurried through to the kitchen where Esme was unpacking the dishwasher from its overnight cycle.

'Were you planning to go to the shops this morning,' he asked innocently.

Esme, who knew that her father detested shopping of all sorts, was immediately suspicious.

'Yes, Dad. Why do you ask?'

'I was just wondering if you're going anywhere near the shops on the eastern side at Rosbury I would appreciate a lift.'

'And why do you want to go there?' Esme asked uneasily.

'Just a call I have to make. Nothing for you to be concerned about.'

'"Nothing for me to be concerned about",' Esme quoted. 'How often have I heard that before. That's what you say when you're about to hare off on another one of your little investigating expeditions. Is this anything to do with Donald's case, because if it is there is no way in the world that I'm going to take you anywhere.'

'Very well. I will make my own way there thank you.'

'And how will you do that? It's too far to walk.'

'I'll take the train,' he said. 'The place I have to visit is close to the station at Rosbury. So don't bother. The walk to the station will do me good.'

'But you haven't answered my question: is it anything to do with Donald's investigation.'

Hodgkiss turned angrily. 'Of course it's to do with Donald's investigation. Someone's got to take these matters seriously ... not simply write people off as narks, bimbos or druggies.

I think Donald's attitude and the attitude of that sergeant were disgraceful.'

'Well I wouldn't argue with that,' Esme conceded. 'Just the same I'm not going to put my neck out by driving you to talk to someone that's going to result in Donald's nose being put out of joint. Sorry, Dad.'

Hodgkiss shook his head. 'No problem, Esme. As I said, I'll take the train.'

*　　*　　*

Rosbury was only one station from Lillimoor and it was less than thirty-five minutes before Hodgkiss found himself standing outside the address Jan Campbell-Jones had read over to him.

It was a block of modern town houses and Hodgkiss pressed the button for number three.

After a short silence a female voice answered.

During the short train trip Hodgkiss had given thought to how he would approach the problem of securing the assistance of anyone in the building prepared to give information about Katie Pye.

He began. 'My name is Edgar Hodgkiss. I don't know who you are but I assume you are a friend of Katie Pye who used to live at this address.'

The voice was curt. 'Yes, this is where Katie lived. What do you want?'

'I am very disturbed at some of the circumstances surrounding Katie's death and I am not satisfied that the police are conducting an efficient inquiry.'

'Nor am I,' said the female voice. 'But what do you think you can do about it? You don't sound like a copper.'

'I am certainly not a copper, but my son-in-law happens to be the investigating officer and I am concerned that his attitude towards this inquiry leaves much to be desired. I hope to acquaint myself with all of the important details of the matter so that I will be in a position to encourage him to take the matter more seriously. Can you help me?'

There was a short pause. 'Yes. I think I can, Mr Hodgkiss. Is your son-in-law that Detective Burke fellow?'

'Yes, I'm afraid so.'

'Then will you come in please.'

There was a buzz and Hodgkiss pushed the door open. He walked into the entry foyer to find a rather attractive young woman standing in the open door of unit three.

'Mr Hodgkiss? Come in,' the young woman stepped aside to let him in. Once inside she held out a hand. 'Jenny Carney.'

Hodgkiss took the hand. 'I'm pleased to meet you, Jenny. I hope I can help.'

'So do I. I must say I wasn't very impressed with your son-in-law's attitude.'

'Oh he's all right really. Just a few rough edges,' said Hodgkiss with a half-hearted attempt at loyalty.

'Rather too many rough edges, I'd say,' said Jenny.

Hodgkiss nodded. 'I wouldn't argue with that.'

Jenny led the way through to the lounge where they settled beside each other on a settee.

Hodgkiss discovered that he still enjoyed the proximity of an attractive young woman.

'Coffee?' she asked.

'Not just now, thank you,' said Hodgkiss. 'Business first if you don't mind.'

'I don't mind at all. Now, what would you like to know?'

Hodgkiss shrugged. 'Everything. My knowledge of events is almost nil. How did you meet Katie in the first place?'

'I just advertised in the local paper for someone to share the rent here. She rang, then came here and we hit it off right from the start. She moved in the next day.'

'You knew where she worked, did you?'

'Oh yes. I was impressed. I thought it must be rather a good job. Interesting.'

'I assume it was you who discovered the body.'

Jenny nodded. 'Yes. I came home. Dumped my bag in the bedroom and came through to make myself a cuppa before bed and there she was, sitting in the armchair in front of the tele.'

Jenny indicated a large wingback chair placed at an angle to the TV screen.

'At first I thought there was nothing wrong ... just that she'd dozed off in front of the television.'

'It was on, was it?'

'No. But I thought she must have turned it off because the remote was next to her on the carpet. Then I realised that she was wearing my clothes.'

'Really?! Did you often do that ... wear each other's clothes?'

'No. Never. We had completely different tastes in clothes. She'd just usually wear a t-shirt and jeans and I had more tailored clothes because of where I work.'

'Which is?'

'An insurance office where we're expected to dress up a bit because sometimes we have to go out to meet clients.'

'And do you remember what clothes she was wearing when she left home last.'

'Yes, I distinctly remember. She had on a T-shirt with the slogan Meat Free on the front and Vegan on the back.'

And was she meat free and a vegan?'

'No. Not at all. She liked wearing it whenever we went out for a hamburger. It was her idea of a joke.'

'And that T-shirt isn't here, or any of the other clothes she was wearing when she went out last.'

'No, but there's an overcoat here … a man's overcoat that I've never seen before.'

Hodgkiss nodded. 'That's what she was wearing when she was brought here.'

'How do you know that? And who brought her?'

'I know that because I've spoken to a lady who saw her being bundled into her car by two men early yesterday morning and she was wearing an overcoat with nothing underneath.'

Jenny shook her head. 'Poor girl. And where was this?'

'In Kryten Street opposite where her boss, the minister, lives. Did you tell Inspector Burke about the clothes not being hers?'

Jenny shook her head vigorously. 'I told him nothing he didn't ask for. I answered his questions and that was all. He really rubbed me up the wrong way.'

'What did he do?'

'He just treated the poor girl like a piece of meat. Just another druggie, that's what he said.'

'Yes, I've heard that from him before. I suppose he asked you if there were any drugs in the flat, did he?'

'Yes. He asked if he could search the place. I told him yes because I knew they'd find nothing. Katie got all her drugs from that fellow she worked for or possibly one of his off-siders.'

Hodgkiss asked. 'And this overcoat you found … do you have it here?'

'Yes. I'll get it for you.' She disappeared into a bedroom next to the kitchen and returned moments later with a dark overcoat.

She handed it to Hodgkiss who immediately began to turn out the pockets.

As he did so a cigarette lighter fell to the carpet.

'What's this?' he said, taking his handkerchief from a pocket and picking up the lighter. 'A cigarette lighter with the initials EW.'

'That'd be her boss … the minister, Evan White.'

'Now, I wonder if the minister has missed his lighter yet. If he's a heavy smoker he must have noticed it missing by now and be wondering where he left it.'

'Then he'll want it back, won't he? He particularly won't want it to be found here.'

'I should say not. Now I think my son-in-law should be informed of this development, don't you? It might encourage him to take the case a little more seriously.'

Jenny shrugged. 'If that's what you think's for the best.'

Hodgkiss reached for his phone and thumbed the keypad.

'Donald I am calling from the home of Jenny Carney whom you know. Yes, that's right, Katie Pye's flat mate. Never mind how I found her address, that is none of your concern. Since arriving here a number of facts have come to my notice that you would do well to follow up. No, I am not about to discuss them over the phone. You must come here without delay. Among other things Ms Carney and I have found a cigarette lighter engraved with initials that will help you progress your investigation to the point where you will in a position to lay charges. Yes, Donald, charges. There is more to this than a simple overdose. You're not interested? Very well. Then perhaps Superintendent O'Hare will be prepared to take me seriously. Yes, of course I have his number. Yes. I thought that might get your attention. I suggest you get here just as quickly as you can. There is a great deal to be done and not much time in which to do it.'

Hodgkiss cut the connection as the intercom sounded.

'I wonder who the hell that can be,' said Jenny. 'I wasn't expecting anyone.'

She crossed to the wall near the front door and pressed the intercom.

'Yes, who is it?'

'My name is Bob Roberts. I work for Mr White, the Minister for Local Government. Katie borrowed one of the minister's overcoats when she left to go home. D'you mind if I come in and get it back? The minister needs it.'

Jenny glanced at Hodgkiss who gave an exaggerated shake of his head.

'No, Mr Roberts, there is no overcoat belonging to Mr White here.'

'I think there is. D'you mind if my friend and I come in to have a look.'

Again Hodgkiss shook his head vigourously.

'Yes, Mr Roberts. I would mind very much. It would not be at all convenient.

The little speaker went dead.

'What now?' Jenny asked uneasily, 'Obviously he knows it's here and I don't imagine he'll give up trying until he's got it back.'

'Is there any way those fellows can get into the building?'

'Not really, unless they can trick one of the others in the building into letting them in and they'd be pretty lucky to find anyone at home at this time of the day. They mostly go out to work.'

Hodgkiss asked. 'Do you have a plastic bag with a seal?'

Jenny nodded, hurried to the kitchen and returned with a clear plastic bag.

'Perfect,' said Hodgkiss dropping the lighter into the bag and closing the seal. 'White could hardly deny it's his with those initials on it, but it's as well to preserve the fingerprints.'

Just then there was a sharp rapping on the unit's front door, then a loud male voice. 'Lady, open up. We need that coat back … now. We know it's in there so don't play silly buggers. We can make you regret it.'

Hodgkiss crossed quickly to the door and slipped the stout safety chain into place. Then he took the phone from his shirt pocket and switched it to camera mode.

He opened the door as far as the chain would permit.

Two large men dressed in dark suits were standing in the hallway immediately outside the door.

Hodgkiss raised the camera which flashed as he took the picture.

'Hey, enough of that,' said one of the men.

'It's not just the coat you're interested in, is it, gentlemen? You're also interested in this, aren't you?'

He held up the clear plastic bag containing the lighter.

'Yeah. So hand it over. It doesn't belong to you.'

'It doesn't belong to you either,' said Hodgkiss. 'Besides, would you care to explain just how the minister's overcoat got here, eh? Would you like to explain that?'

When neither of the men offered an explanation, Hodgkiss suggested: 'You used it to cover Katie Pye who had no clothes on when you brought her here.'

One of the men raised a hand and pointed directly at Hodgkiss. 'Hey, I know you. You're the guy we saw talking to the old troublemaking bitch from the flats opposite when we arrived yesterday morning? Yeah, I'm sure it was you. Now listen, we can make all sorts of trouble for you if you don't give us back those things of the boss's now.'

Hodgkiss shook his head. 'Those things belonging to your boss will be going straight to the police officer who is in charge of this case. We are expecting him to arrive here at any moment. So tell your boss that,' Hodgkiss said, confident in the chain and door between him and the men.

One of the men stepped forward and slammed his shoulder against the door, but the chain held.

Hodgkiss attempted to close door but found a large, scruffy boot had been inserted between the door and the jamb. He turned his back, raised his right leg and brought down the heel of his shoe heavily on the top of the intruding boot cap.

There was a squeal of pain and the boot was hastily withdrawn.

Hodgkiss closed the door firmly, leaving the chain in place.

'Now what?' Jenny asked. 'I doubt if we've seen the last of those two beauties.'

She hurried through to the front of the unit. 'They're leaving now.' She called. 'But I expect they'll be back soon.'

It was little more than a minute before there was another knock on the door.

'Who is it?' Hodgkiss demanded.'

'Who do you think it is?' came Donald's voice. 'The Good Fairy?'

'How did you get into the building, Donald?'

'There were two blokes just leaving as I arrived. I came in as they came out.'

'Then I hope you had a good look at them so you will recognise them again.'

'Oh, and why is that?'

'Because you will be arresting them shortly.'

A short pause. 'Are you going to let me in or not?'

Hodgkiss removed the safety chain and opened the door.

Before Donald had even crossed the threshold Hodgkiss warned: 'And this time, when you address Ms Carney, I suggest you use more sensitive and respectful language than you did when last you were here.'

Donald ignored this sally. He nodded towards Jenny then turned to Hodgkiss. 'OK. Now what are these fact you mentioned that I need to know?"

'I suggest you ask Ms Carney here. She has all of the information you require to bring this tragic matter to a successful conclusion.'

'I've already spoken to Ms Carney once and she had no facts likely to take me anywhere. In fact Ms Carney was not at all helpful.'

'And have you any idea why that was?'

'I assume she had nothing worthwhile to say or she's got something to hide.'

'Well you assumed wrongly, Donald, as you frequently do. Now, I suggest you address your questions to Ms Carney again, but more respectfully this time.'

'I already asked her if she had any idea how her friend died, did she know Ms Pye was a druggie, where she kept the drugs ... she played dumb. Didn't know anything.' He turned to Jenny. 'Isn't that true. You said you didn't know anything about how or where your friend got her drugs.'

'Yes, and it's true. I don't.'

'OK, then let's start from the beginning and get some facts. What time did you arrive home and find your flat mate dead?'

'Around two. A little before perhaps.'

Hodgkiss sighed and shook his head. 'Donald, there are

far more important matters to be investigated than when Ms Pye was found.'

'Oh? F'rinstance?'

'Well a good starting point would be to ask the question why was Ms Pye wearing Jenny's clothes when she was found?'

'Ms Carney never told me anything about the other girl wearing her clothes.'

'Well, if you ask her now, politely, she just might tell you.'

Donald took a deep breath, then turned to Jenny. 'Is it true Ms Pye was wearing your clothes when you found her?'

Jenny nodded. 'Yes, she was. And I can tell you something else; she didn't put them on herself.'

'Oh. And how do you know that?'

'Well, first of all she was wearing one of my bras. I've never known Katie to wear a bra as long as I've known her. Secondly, whoever dressed her put my top on her inside out. Usually clothes have the maker's label on the inside, but some designer clothes have the labels to be worn on the outside. If Katie put my top on she would have known that and put it on with the label showing at the back. And another thing; I can't find anywhere any of the clothes she was wearing when she left home in the morning.'

'And you know what that means, don't you Donald,' said Hodgkiss.

Donald frowned. 'You mean she wasn't wearing any of her clothes when she came home. But that's nonsense. She must have had something on.'

'Yes,' said Hodgkiss, pointing. 'She was wearing that overcoat … and nothing else.'

'And how do you know that?'

'I know that because the lady in the flats opposite saw her wearing that and nothing else the night she died, and secondly because the owner of that overcoat has sent his uncouth agents to retrieve it. They were the two men you saw leaving the building as you entered. But the overcoat was not the only item they came to retrieve. They wanted this too.'

Hodgkiss held up the plastic bag containing the cigarette lighter.

'And what's that?'

'This, Donald, is a cigarette lighter belonging to one Evan White.'

'Evan White. Isn't he something in the government?' Donald asked.

'He is the Minister for Local Government.'

'And how on earth does he come into the picture?'

'Katie Pye was an employee in his ministerial office … and no doubt also his mistress. She was seen being removed, naked except for that overcoat, from the minister's home in the early hours of the morning. She was brought here by the minister's agents who decided, surprisingly, to dress her. However, unwittingly they dressed her in Jenny's clothes. I'm sure you will find the fingerprints of those people on many of the surfaces here, so why don't you call the scene-of-crime officers and get the process started now. You know as well as I, Donald, that the sooner an investigation commences after the commission of a crime the greater are the chances of a successful outcome.'

'So what if we do find some fingerprints. What are we going to charge these guys with?' He turned to Jenny. 'Did they break into the place?'

Jenny shook her head. 'No. I didn't notice anything like that. I suppose they used Katie's keys to get in. They would have been on the key ring with her car keys.'

Hodgkiss shook his head in dismay. 'Donald, do you really mean to tell me that no criminal offence has been committed here; that you can think of no charges to bring against those men. Is it all right to carry dead bodies around the suburbs at night? Who gave her the drugs that killed her? Was there any attempt to get medical help for her?'

Donald nodded and took out his mobile phone.

*   *   *

Bob and Frank stood, heads hanging, in front of the minister in his suite in Macquarie Street. The office was on the north-eastern corner, thirty levels up, with views of the Opera House and the Bridge.

Bob explained. 'We couldn't get in. The overcoat's there all right, it's gotta be unless they got rid of it. And they've got the lighter too. The old bugger in there with the girl even showed it to me. He had it in a plastic bag.'

'In a plastic bag,' the minister repeated thoughtfully. 'Now, tell me everything that happened … from the top.'

'Well we got there and Frank buzzed the girl's unit. She answered and we said who we were and that we just wanted to collect the overcoat. Real friendly. She reckoned it wasn't there and hung up on us.

'When she wouldn't open the door to let us into the building I got out the old credit card and got us into the foyer. Of course we knew which one was the unit so I knocked on the door and asked could we just come in and get the overcoat. I was very polite. Anyway the girl wouldn't let us in.

'Then suddenly the door opened a bit with the safety chain on. Then this old guy I'd seen before looks out around the door and what does he do … he takes a bloody photo of us with his bloody phone.'

The minister summarized. 'So not only have you not got

the coat and lighter back but you've had your photos taken so you can be identified.'

'But what does it matter,' said Bob. 'We haven't done anything wrong. The cops've nothing on us. And another thing … I've found out who that old guy is. His name's Edgar Hodgkiss. I remembered that I'd seen him a couple of times up at the council chambers when I was up there doing jobs for you in the planning department. I asked one of the fellows there did they know anything about him. As soon as I described him they knew who I meant on account of the little beard. He's a real trouble maker.'

The minister asked. 'And he was holding my lighter in a plastic bag, was he?'

Frank nodded eagerly. 'Yeah. That's right.'

The minister nodded. 'Yeah. Well, thanks boys. Take the rest of the day off.'

When Bob and Frank had departed Evan picked up the phone to his private secretary in the office outside.

'Get me the Minister for Police and Justice. And I mean now. Tell him it's urgent.'

*   *   *

Next morning Hodgkiss was slumped in one of the director's chairs on the back deck when he heard the sound of a car door slamming in the driveway.

Moments later Donald appeared at the foot of the short flight of wooden stairs leading up to the deck.

'What brings you home at this hour?' Hodgkiss asked, glancing at his watch which showed eleven. 'I thought you'd have plenty to do today following up on the dreadful business about that girl.'

Donald pulled out one of the curved benches around the redwood table and sat. 'Yeah. So did I, but the super had other ideas.'

Hodgkiss sat up. 'Just what do you mean by that ... what other ideas did Superintendent O'Hare have?'

'Well, I was just on my way to parliament house to ask Minister White a few questions about the girl and what'd happened to her when O'Hare got on the blower and told me to leave him alone and to take the morning off.'

'And what reason did he give for telling you that?'

Donald shrugged. 'He said something about the police not being allowed to question politicians inside parliament house.'

'First I've heard of that,' said Hodgkiss. 'But I suppose that can be put on hold for the time being. What have the medical people had to say about her?'

'They haven't done an autopsy yet but the doctor said there's no doubt she died of an overdose. All the classical symptoms are there.'

'No doubt, but the important questions is where did she die. Could the doctor tell you anything about the time of death?'

'Only the usual wide range ... between ten at night and two in the morning.'

'Well, seeing that Jenny found her about two it's more likely than not that she was dead before she was brought to the unit.'

'Yeah, and the doctor commented on a cut on her left arm. He said it had been done very recently but after she'd died because it hardly bled.'

Hodgkiss said: 'Then it's highly likely that the girl sustained the injury when those fellows dropped her on the road while carrying her to the car to drive her home.'

Donald nodded. 'Yeah. There were traces of blood on the

inside of the sleeve of the overcoat she had on and the blood was in the sleeve where she'd been hurt.'

'Then one is driven ineluctably to the conclusion that Ms Pye died of the overdose at the minister's home and he was having his uncouth henchmen remove her so that no one would suspect she died of an overdose while in his company, wouldn't you say?'

'Not much doubt about it, Dad. The problem is getting to talk to him.'

'He can't stay holed-up in parliament house for ever, can he? He'll have to come out and go home some time.'

'Yeah. But that's another problem. Superintendent O'Hare said to clear it with him before I try to set up an interview with the guy … even at his home or anywhere else.'

Hodgkiss frowned. 'Did he? That is most disturbing. I would hate to think that somehow the superintendent had been influenced to protect this fellow.'

'So would I. Nothing like that's ever happened before. I know for a fact the super's resisted some pretty heavy political pressure in the past. He hates it when politicians try to put the screws on him. I haven't even told him yet about the results of the fingerprint checks from the girls unit. One of the minister's men left his dabs all over the place. Fellow called Bob Roberts. He's got quite a record going back years. Why they'd have a bloke like that working on a minister's staff I'd never know.'

Just then they were disturbed by the sound of hurried footsteps in the driveway. Moments later Esme appeared, breathless, at the bottom of the stairs.

'What's up with you?' Donald asked. 'What's the rush? Do you want me to move my car out of the driveway so you can come in?'

Esme shook her head impatiently. 'No. I've been followed around all morning by two men in a car?'

'What?' said Donald, coming to his feet.

'Hurry and I'll show you. They're still parked down the road.'

Esme turned and almost ran back down the driveway towards the street, Donald and Hodgkiss hard on her heels.

When they reached the front of the house Esme pointed. 'There, that big dark car parked outside the Wentworth's place. It was there this morning when I left for the shops and as soon as I drove away it started up and followed. It drove up very close behind me ... too close for comfort. I really felt quite frightened. When I parked at the railway station car park at Grattan they drove in and parked near me.'

'And did they follow you into the shops?' Donald asked.

'No, but they were still sitting in the car when I came back and they followed me all the way back here ... tailgating me all the way.'

'Did they indeed,' said Donald, setting off quickly in the direction of the parked car.

But Donald had not gone more than a few paces when the car started up. made a quick U turn and disappeared in the opposite direction.

'I got their number,' said Esme.

'Good work,' said Hodgkiss. 'I've no doubt those were the two fellows who took Ms Pye's body back to her unit. This is another example of how determined they are to prevent a proper investigation of this matter. Now they resort to blatant intimidation. Very nasty.'

As they hurried back down the driveway towards the back deck Donald took out his mobile phone and thumbed the key pad.

'Superintendent, it's Burke here. I thought you ought to know those two goons who moved the girl's body out of that politician's house have been following Esme around in their car trying to intimidate her. Yes, of course she's sure. She said it's the same two fellows she saw driving the car that turned into the minister's place. She got a good look at them. So what are we going to do about that. Is it OK if I have a word with them now? Yes, at the minister's place because that's probably where they've gone now. But superintendent, we can't just let them carry on like this. It's not like you to pull the blind down. What's happened? I don't know what to think about it, but I know we can't just let all this go through to the keeper. There's no doubt that the poor girl died at that fellow's place. Of course I can prove it. The timing's right, the doctor said so, and Dad agrees that it's got to be that way. The cut on her arm didn't bleed when they dropped her outside the house and that means she was already dead. OK. Then we can talk more about it tomorrow, but we can't hold off just because the guy's got connections.'

He listened briefly then cut the connection without another word.

'Someone's really scared the living daylights out of him,' said Donald as he returned the phone to his shirt pocket.

Esme said. 'Well I can't go out to the shops and have those fellows following me everywhere.'

'No,' said Hodgkiss. 'That cannot be allowed to continue. Now, if the superintendent is unable to allow Donald to prosecute this inquiry then another way must be found and … as the old saying goes … there's more than one way to skin a cat.'

Esme and Donald turned to look at Hodgkiss, anxiety written plainly on their faces.

'Now Dad,' Esme began. 'What do you mean by that? What have you got in mind?'

'What I have in mind, my girl, is to make sure that you are no longer troubled by the minister's bully boys, and since Donald is not permitted to continue his investigation then other ways must be found of seeing that the pertinent questions arising from this tragic series of events are asked and answered.'

'And how do you plan to do that?' Donald demanded.

Hodgkiss laid a finger against the side of the nose. 'Leave it to me. Remember that other old saying … ask no questions and you'll be told no lies.'

Hodgkiss pulled back the heavy sliding door to the family room and hurried to his bedroom at the front of the house.

He closed the door and took out his phone.

*　　*　　*

Roger Carpenter's contact in the town planning department at Kanundda Council was a man with interesting connections.

The contact, Alf Newton, had a cousin in the police, Constable Ken Williams, who was stationed at Grattan, where he heard all of the gossip that circulated around the various patrols on the North Shore.

A truly juicy morsel had come Constable Williams's way and he lost no time passing it on to Cousin Alf at the Kanundda Council.

Cousin Alf, in turn, lost no time in passing it on to Roger Carpenter who paid for information of this nature and importance, if not in cash, then in kind; a case or two of rather nice wine was one way that Roger Carpenter showed his appreciation.

And this was a very juicy morsel indeed … certainly a two-case snippet.

At first Roger could scarcely believe his ears as Cousin Alf unpacked the nitty-gritty of the morsel. 'Guess who was called into parliament house to cop a dressing down? None other than Superintendent O'Hare. My information is that when he arrived they took him to one of the conference rooms in the Premier's suite and one of the Premier's men and the Minister for Police and Justice were sitting there waiting for him. Poor old O'Hare never got a word in. They told him that he was to stop his detective at Crestwood, that'd be Donald Burke, from harassing Minister White. They told O'Hare that his people did not have a skerrick of evidence that White had anything to do with the death of the girl who used to work in his office and that if there was any more complaints from Minister White about Burke wanting to interview him or anyone connected with him it would be the end of Superintendent O'Hare's career. He'd find himself at a one-man station back of Bourke.'

'They reckon when O'Hare left he was white and shaking. He had to go to the hotel over the road to steady his nerves.'

Carpenter thanked Cousin Alf and made a mental note to send two cases of best Burgundy.

He did not doubt for one moment that the information was correct and the more he thought about it the less he liked it.

Things were getting more than a little out of hand if the Premier's people had to intervene in order to derail a police investigation.

Events such as that were not easily buried and the indignities visited upon those involved were not readily forgotten or forgiven.

Carpenter had a nasty feeling that this drastic step would

eventually come back to bite those involved and he did not intend to be anywhere around when the teeth went in.

He picked up his phone and punched in the numbers for the office of the Minister for Local Government.

When he was finally put through to the minister he did not mince words.

'Mate, I've heard about the Premier and your mate the Minister for Police trying to sit on the thing about that girl of yours who died.

'It won't work, believe me. So I'm pulling the pin.'

'Pulling the pin,' the minister repeated, incredulous. 'What do you mean, pulling the pin.'

'I'm call off the St James job. I don't like the way things are shaping up. It's not going to be worth the hassle.'

Minister White was not pleased. His wife already had spent most of the anticipated profits from the project. 'I'll get my money back then?'

'Yeah, of course … in time. There's one or two things got to be sorted out first. None of us'll get all of our stake back because there's already been expenses and we'll all have to bear the cost of them.'

'Expenses! What are you talking about? You never even turned a sod.'

'Maybe not. But there were detailed plans prepared which meant architects have been paid … and they're not cheap. And we had to pay a few fellahs at council to get the plans prioritized and make sure they'd get approved.'

Evan protested. 'But they never even bloody went to council.'

'No, they didn't, but they were ready to go and the guys were going to recommend in favour of them although they didn't really measure up.

'Then there were a couple of councillors who had to be kept happy because they were worried the plans weren't quite up to scratch ... and they weren't cheap.'

'So I've done my dough cold, is that it?'

'Oh no. You'll get something back.'

Minister White cut the connection savagely.

'Crooks,' he muttered. 'I'm surrounded by bloody crooks.'

Carpenter ended the call with a strong feeling of unease. Dealing with guys like White who could not deliver their side of a bargain on time was bad for business.

The present delay in getting the job started was not going to be sheeted home to him.

He got Cousin Alf back on the line.

He said: 'Alf, I've had to call off that big St James job because bloody White couldn't get his act together to fix the approvals we needed. I'd like you to put it around your mates in the industry that pulling the job is because of White ... couldn't be relied on to do his bit. I wouldn't like the men with the money to think that I'm a fellah who can't get a job done.'

Cousin Alf smiled. 'I get the picture. The job went down because he couldn't be relied on. Nothing to do with you. You were ready to go.'

'That's the picture, Alf,' said Carpenter. 'And it also happens to be true ... mostly.'

*   *   *

While Minister White was taking the unwelcome call from Carpenter another call was being made which would have even more dire consequences for the minister.

In his office at the Daily News reporter Kevin Spruce cursed as his mobile phone rang.

He had just started writing a story critical of the State Government's *laissez faire* attitude towards local government matters, so the interruption was not welcome.

He reached for the phone. He decided not to take the call unless it was from one of his regular contacts.

He glanced at the screen where the name Hodgkiss was displayed.

Kevin smiled. Hodgkiss had been his English teacher throughout secondary school. He hesitated then opened the connection.

'Hi Edgar, how's tricks. Good to hear from you. What have you got for me?'

'That's what I've always liked about you, Kevin. Straight to the point.'

'I need to be. I'm on a deadline at the moment for my latest story.'

'Oh, and which branch of Government will be on the receiving end this time?'

'Local Government ... the third tier as it coyly calls itself.'

'Now there's a happy conjunction of the stars. My call happens to be about local government, or more particularly the Minister for Local Government.'

'Really. Then you have my full attention, Edgar. I've heard too many bad stories about that fellow for them all to be wrong.'

'Well here's another one you can add to your collection and this one, you may be sure, is perfectly true.'

'OK, Edgar,' said Kevin. 'Unload.'

Hodgkiss began. 'Two nights ago a young woman by the name of Katie Pye ...'

'Word around the traps is she's his girlfriend,' said Kevin.

'*Was* his girl friend. The young woman is unfortunately deceased. She died of a drugs overdose at his home.'

'Edgar, how do you know this?'

'My son-in-law, Detective Inspector Donald Burke, who is stationed at Crestwood, is investigating the death. Or rather *was* investigating it. He has been called off. His superior, Superintendent O'Hare, hitherto a very upright and straight police officer, was summoned to parliament house where he was instructed to order Donald to stop the investigation. Accordingly Donald was told he could not go to parliament house to interview the minister and he was told also not to interview the minister at home or anywhere without clearing it with the superintendent.'

'Hold it, Edgar,' said. 'What you are saying is that there's two stories here. The clamp down on the investigation and Katie Pye dying at the minister's home.'

'Yes I suppose you could say there are two for the price of one,' said Hodgkiss. 'Now, may I continue.'

'Go for it.'

'We know that Ms Pye died at the minister's home because she was already dead when two of the minister's goons carried her out to her car which was parked opposite. Before they managed to load her into the car they dropped her onto the roadway injuring an arm.'

'How do you know all this, Edgar. Were you actually there?'

'No, unfortunately, but I spoke to a lady who lives directly opposite. She saw the whole thing. Her name is Phyllis Thomson, without a P, and she will confirm what I have said. Her number is in the book. When you ring her you may tell her you have spoken to me.

'Now, to continue; the police doctor noted that the injury to Ms Pye's arm had been inflicted after death because there was very little bleeding. That is borne out by the condition of the minister's overcoat in which they had dressed her.

There was almost no trace of blood on the lining of the coat corresponding to the position of the injury.'

Kevin asked. 'But why was she wearing an overcoat? It was quite a warm night.'

'An excellent question, Kevin. She was wearing his overcoat because they didn't want to carry her naked over the road to her car.'

Kevin chuckled. 'I getcha. So they'd been at it.'

'So it would appear. But it gets worse ... or better from your story's point of view. These two goons delivered her home to her unit. They had her keys so they could take her inside without any bother. Luckily for them her flat mate was out at the time which was then shortly before 2 a.m. Her flat mate arrived shortly afterwards and found Ms Pye's body sitting propped up in an arm chair in front of the television ... fully clothed.

'It appears that the two goons, having delivered Ms Pye, took it into their heads to dress her. No doubt they intended to return the minister's overcoat and did not wish to leave the unfortunate girl just sitting around naked.

'But when they dressed her it was not in her own clothes. Unwittingly they dressed her in her flat mate's clothes. An understandable mistake in the circumstances. They were not to know which clothes hanging around in the various wardrobes belonged to which girl.

'However in the end they left the overcoat behind and in one of its pockets was a cigarette lighter with the initials EW, and of course one doesn't not have to think long and hard to put a name to EW.

'Evan White.'

'Obviously.'

'That is some story, Edgar.'

'Wait. There's more. These two prize goons happened to

see Esme, Ms Thomson and I in Esme's car the next morning when they arrived at the minister's place.

'They slowed down and had a good look at us as they turned in.

'They knew that Ms Thomson had been on her deck in the middle of the night and had witnessed the whole awful procession from the minister's front door until they had placed Ms Pye in her own vehicle and driven away.

'Somehow they traced ownership of Esme's car and assuming no doubt that Ms Thomson had told Esme of what she saw, they got it into their fat heads that they should deter Esme from discussing their activities with anyone.

'So what do they do? They follow her when she drives to the shops. They tailgate her on the way home.

'Then when Donald approaches them when they are parked out in the street they take off like scalded cats.'

'That is the broad outline of events. You will have little difficulty filling in the details.

'I suspect that the most telling part of your story will be the minister's reaction when you put the facts to him ... or attempt to.'

Kevin said: 'I expect he'll deny everything of course even if he agrees to talk to me, which I doubt. I'll have a talk to the Premier's office too about them heavying the superintendent from Crestwood. Of course they'll deny that too. But our readers will quite rightly take their denials as admissions. These people always deny things until it's obvious they've lied then they try to think of some way to wriggle out or cover up and the cover up always gets them into more trouble than the original story.

'I'll start making calls now and let you know how I make out.'

Hodgkiss chuckled. 'Happy hunting,' he said and cut the connection.

*   *   *

The Premier, like Queen Victoria, was not amused.

He had just sacked his assistant private secretary, a promising young stalwart from his party's head office who had been given the job as reward for his hard work in the lead up to the successful campaign at the last elections..

He sighed. He knew the sacking would bring down trouble on his head from the left faction, but he'd had no choice. The young idiot, and that bigger idiot, the Minister for Police and Justice, who should have known better, had actually heavied a superintendent of police to call off an investigation into the death of one of Evan White's staffers, a sexy little piece he'd noticed floating around the corridors of parliament house.

And as if all that wasn't bad enough, now the bloody media was onto it. Kevin Someone from the News had rung wanting to speak to him about that girl's death and suggesting the minister was involved. He'd got his press secretary to fob the fellow off, saying he knew nothing about it which was not strictly true, but then you didn't make press statements under oath.

But he'd have to find out from bloody Evan White what had actually happened and if that slimy bastard tried to pull the wool he'd have his job.

He was about to summon White to his office when his private secretary, Beth Capper, a tall woman of middle years with a deep voice, came in and turned on the large wall-mounted TV set opposite his desk.

Immediately an image of Katie Pye dressed alluringly in a bikini appeared on the screen.

'The News On Line Edition' the private secretary explained.

The voice of the reporter was saying: 'An eyewitness who lives opposite says she saw two men who appeared to be supporting a third person come out of the house. As they approached a small red car parked outside one of the men dropped the person he was trying to support onto the road. It was then that the eyewitness realised it was a woman who had been dropped because she was wearing only an overcoat which fell open when she fell. The two men put her in the car and one of them drove off with the girl and the other followed in a second car.'

'The News has attempted to contact the office of the Minister for Local Government where Ms Pye worked, but the minister has declined to comment.'

'I'll bet he has,' said the Premier. 'Turn that thing off, Beth, and get that idiot in here.'

Minutes later Beth was on the line. 'The Minister for Local Government is out of his office and cannot be contacted.'

The Premier shook his head. 'Now there's a surprise. But he won't be able to duck and weave for ever. Tell his office I want to talk to him now and stress the now and suggest dire consequences if he's not here in my office within thirty minutes.'

The Minister for Local Government, it turned out was actually in his office and had to travel only three levels in the elevator to reach the Premier's suite on the top floor of the Governor Bligh Towers.

'But Premier,' he protested, 'I couldn't report it. Next thing the coroner, the cops, the whole shooting match would have been swarming all over the house.'

The Premier was not sympathetic. 'And they might have found something they shouldn't have, isn't that right? If she died of an overdose, which seems to be the case, chances are she took the stuff at your place and other chances are she kept her stuff there too, so I can understand why you didn't want the cops crawling all over the place. But Evan, moving a dead body … what possessed you to do that. I'm no lawyer but it seems to me that there must be a law against that. What do you reckon?'

'Yeah, I don't know either and maybe there is. But no way could I have her found there. The media would have had a field day.'

'So what do you think they're going to do now? Forget about it? I don't think so. And you put her in your overcoat and one of your goons dropped her on the road. How's that going to look. Poor kid had nothing on under the coat according to a woman who saw the whole bloody charade. It's not looking good for you from where I'm sitting. Have you thought about what you're going to say when the media catches up with you, as they will?'

'Yeah. I've thought about it and I'm going to deny the whole thing.'

'What? Say that it never happened?'

'Why not? The only person that actually saw anything was one old bat who lives over the road and she's got it in for me anyway. I reckon I can handle that.'

The Premier stood. 'OK, Evan. You handle it then. But if this story is still running in a day or two I'm going to have to drop you over the side. Understood?'

'Don't worry Premier. I can handle it.'

'And this time it'd be a good idea if you handled it yourself and not leave it to those two goons who dropped the girl on the road.'

*   *   *

Minister White had no sooner left the Premier's office that Beth Capper buzzed to inform the premier that the Member for Kanundda, Olly Bryant, an ambitious back-bencher was on the line.

'Put him through, Beth,' said the Premier. 'Got to keep the back bench happy. Yes, Olly what's new?'

The Premier listened with growing concern. 'You sure of that, Olly. Looks bad if true. Yes, I'm sure you haven't made it up. Thanks, I'll look into it.'

As soon as he'd hung up the Premier buzzed the intercom and Beth appeared again. 'Olly said there's a story doing the rounds that bloody White had some deal going with a builder name of Carpenter. The arrangement was that White was going to over-rule the Kanundda Council on some zoning changes so his mate could get on with the job. Will you ask around and get the Whip onto it. We don't want stories like that doing the rounds.

Less than an hour later Beth Capper again interrupted the Premier who had thought he might be able to grab a few minutes free for a quick snifter.

Without a word she turned on the television again, this time with the sound muted. 'This is an update on the story about Minister White.'

The screen showed a suburban brick bungalow. Beth explained. 'That's where the copper lives who White called off the case. The lady being interviewed is the copper's wife.'

She turned off the mute.

The woman was mid-sentence: " … and they followed me home in their big car, tailgating me all the way. I've got only a little car and I felt very intimidated. When I got home I went straight in and told my husband who was at home because he'd been ordered not to investigate the matter any more. And of course he went straight out into the street to tell these fellows off. But as soon as they saw him they took of like a scalded cat.'

The camera drew back to take in the interviewer. He asked. 'And do you know who was driving the other car that followed you, Mrs Burke.'

'Oh yes, I'd know those two anywhere. I saw them very recently driving into the house where that Minister Mr White lives. The lady who lives over the road saw the two of them carrying that poor girl out after she'd died in the minister's house from an overdose of drugs.'

'Turn it off,' the Premier snapped. 'That's the last straw. That and the deal with the builder fellow ... getting his fingers dirty in some grubby little local government planning scam. He's got to go. Ring the bastard now and tell him I want his letter of resignation by five this evening. And send in my press secretary. I want a statement for the six o'clock news about White resigning to spend more time with his family.'

*　　*　　*

'As soon as I heard the guy had been sacked I told Donald to go get him.'

Superintendent O'Hare had levered his bulk into one side of the breakfast nook, his broad Irish features animated.

He turned to Donald who was standing by the sink helping Esme prepare morning tea. 'And I reckon you've done a pretty good job.'

'A pretty good job so far,' put in Hodgkiss who was seated

opposite O'Hare. 'There's still a lot more work to be done to bring all of those disgusting people to justice.'

'Oh, no doubt about that, Edgar,' said O'Hare, who had great respect for Hodgkiss' opinion.

Hodgkiss continued. 'And at the top of the list are those two arrogant criminals who sought to intimidate you, superintendent.'

'Well the premier sacked one of them on the spot,' said O'Hare.

'Yes, and there's a lesson to be learned from that.'

'And what lesson is that Oh Great Wise One?' Donald asked.

'Need you ask, Donald? I would have thought it was obvious.'

'There you go again, Dad,' said Esme angrily. 'Saying something's obvious … meaning you're the only one smart enough to see it.'

'That's not what I meant at all,' said Hodgkiss.

'Of course it is,' said Donald, smelling blood and joining battle. . 'You're always saying how obvious things are. You just love putting people down and making out how smart you are.'

Hodgkiss mounted a spirited defense and the argument rolled on.

Hodgkiss and Death at the Wicket

'**D**ad, would you mind taking your book out on the back deck or maybe to your bedroom. I'll be turning on the TV in a couple of minutes. The cricket's just about to start.'

Donald Burke, aware of his father-in-law's propensity to create a confrontation over even the most trifling domestic situations, made his request in the most conciliatory tones he could manage.

But he needn't have bothered.

Edgar Hodgkiss was spoiling for a fight.

Hodgkiss looked up sharply from his paperback novel. 'If you want to watch the cricket I suggest you watch it on the set in your bedroom, like you have for the last umpteen years. I was here first. Besides, the sun will have gone off the back deck by now and it'll be chilly out there. And I spend half my life in the bedroom as it is without going there to read.' He raised the book and continued reading.

Donald closed his eyes and gritted his teeth. 'Now look,

Dad, we agreed to buy a new tele with a big screen specially for watching sport, so what'd be the point of me going to watch it on the tiny set in the bedroom?'

Hodgkiss shrugged. 'Really, Donald, that's your problem. This is by far the best place for me to read; right here, with my back to the light.'

He lowered his eyes to the page once more.

Donald had had enough.

'And what's that ruddy book you've got your nose in now? Another one of those silly mysteries, is it?'

When Hodgkiss failed to take the bait Donald pressed on.

'Honestly, I don't know what you see in those silly stories. Most of them are so far-fetched they're out of sight. The sort of thing that happens in some of them would never happen in real life. You'd have to admit that.'

Hodgkiss turned a page.

Donald offered an example. 'I mean, whoever heard of a whole gang of people lining up to stab the one bloke … and on board a train, too, with guards and passengers everywhere. I've never heard of anything so ridiculous. Are you going to sit there and tell me that something like that could actually happen?'

When it became apparent that Hodgkiss was not about to tell him anything of the sort Donald continued.

'And what about the one we watched on tele the other night; the one that happened on a ferry or whatever it was, where the girl pretended to shoot her boyfriend in the leg so everyone would think that he couldn't possibly have run around the deck to his wife's cabin to shot her and then he really shot himself in the leg later. Talk about far-fetched!'

When this further example failed to rouse Hodgkiss to a

defence, Donald searched his memory for further examples of the improbable in detective fiction.

'And what about that other one where the killer lowered a dummy or a mask or something to make the victim look out of their window so he could drop a ruddy great rock on his head.'

Hodgkiss didn't look up. 'On *her* head, actually.'

'His head ... her head. What does it matter? The whole thing was ridiculous. I mean, nobody is going to even try something as dopey as that ... not in real life. Even you'd have to admit that.'

'Would I? I don't think so.'

'But Dad, surely you don't really think ...'

But Hodgkiss had had enough. 'Donald, answer me this: how many times in the past several years have you come home from a crime scene and assured me that the victim must have committed suicide simply because the body was found in a room with the door and windows locked and bolted? Answer me that.'

Before Donald could venture a reply Hodgkiss continued. 'Even I couldn't tell you because I have lost count. But I can remember you scoffing at me on numerous occasions when I cautioned you not to accept such a scenario as *prima face* evidence of suicide.'

Donald conceded. 'Yes, Dad. I have to agree you've been right about that more than once. But guys shooting themselves in the leg and half a dozen villains on a train lining up to take turns to stab a guy ... c'mon now, even you've got to admit that plots like that are pretty far fetched.'

Hodgkiss sighed. 'Yes, Donald, of course they're far fetched. But the problem with you is that you fail to enter into the spirit of the classic whodunit, and by failing to do so you deny yourself the pleasure that this genre has given to countless millions around the world for the best part of a century. Actually, I pity you.'

'Well, I don't want your pity, Dad. I just want you to move so I can watch the ruddy cricket.' Then he added with exaggerated politeness. 'If you wouldn't mind.'

Hodgkiss closed his book and wriggled out of the deep chair. 'Don't over do it, Donald.'

Donald picked up the remote and thumbed the set to life. 'Anyway, Dad, you enjoy watching cricket, don't you, so why don't you come out to the match tomorrow with Esme and me? Inspector O'Hare will be meeting us out there. You and the inspector get along fine. I'm sure he'd be pleased to see you.'

Inspector O'Hare, Donald's superior officer at the nearby Crestwood Police Station, was one of the few people outside the Burke household who knew the extent of Hodgkiss's contributions to the sometimes spectacular solutions to many of Donald's investigations.

'Thank you for the invitation, Donald,' said Hodgkiss, heading for the door, 'but as it happens I'm going to Pat's tomorrow to watch the game with her. Kindly give my regards to the inspector.'

As he walked down the hall towards his bedroom at the front of the house Hodgkiss heard his mobile phone begin to ring. He knew at once that the caller could be one of only two people since he had given out his number to very few. In fact the only people who knew his number, other than Donald and Esme, were Pat Strong, with whom he had enjoyed a close personal relationship over several years, and Jan Campbell-Jones, the general manager of the Kanundda Council, the local government body responsible for the well-being of citizens living in those suburbs, including Lillimoor where the Burke's home was to be found.

Over the years of their association, Jan and Hodgkiss had developed a close rapport. This bond grew from a shared determination to protect the interests of the ratepayers of Kanundda from the perils posed by members of a local council which too often comprised men and women who held self-enrichment as their guiding principle, and the well-being of ratepayers trailing in a distant second place.

Hodgkiss picked up his mobile phone from the bedside table and glanced at the caller's number as he settled on the end of the bed.

'Good morning, Jan. And to what do I owe the pleasure of this call?'

Seated at the desk in her spacious but Spartan office at the front of the Kanundda Council Chambers building at the nearby Grattan shopping village, Jan Campbell-Jones swung her ergonomic chair to one side and extended her long, elegant legs towards the centre of the room.

'Good morning, Hodgkiss. Now, don't get your hopes up. I have no fresh examples of municipal double-dealings to report; no evidence of new corruption or treachery to make your day. Instead I have an invitation for you. If you're free tomorrow morning I thought you might like to join me for coffee.'

'As you know I am always delighted to join you for coffee, madam general manager, however tomorrow morning I have a prior engagement with Pat Strong to watch the cricket at her place.'

'Lucky Pat Strong. I trust that cricket-viewing will be the only indoor sporting activity the two of you are likely to engage in.'

Hodgkiss chuckled. 'I can't make any promises about that. Maybe you and I can meet for coffee the following day.'

'Yes, no problem there. It's just that tomorrow I'll be meeting someone you may have found particularly interesting.'

Intrigued, Hodgkiss rose and crossed to the desk in front of the room's only window which looked out over the front garden with its weed-flecked lawn and unkempt garden beds. 'Oh. And who's this someone I might have found particularly interesting?'

'It's a lady who is also extremely interested in cricket. She used to play for the state in her younger days but now she is involved in the game as an administrator. I understand her late husband was quite a well-known player. That's as much as I can tell you. I'm not really much into cricket or sport generally.'

'So why do you think this particular cricket-administering lady would be of particular interest to me?' Hodgkiss asked.

'Because of her intimate knowledge of the shady side of the game,' said Jan. 'I thought that'd be right up your alley.'

'The shady side of cricket! I don't think I've heard a great deal about that aspect of the sport.'

'Have you never heard of gambling, Hodgkiss, particularly as it relates to players from the Indian Sub-continent?'

'Oh yes. I've heard about that of course. Everyone's heard about that. You could hardly fail to. But of course I know only what I've read in the papers and that's probably only half the story. But I can't say that I've ever read much about the gambling disease infecting cricket matches in this country.'

'Then this lady would be able to fill the deficit in your knowledge which seems to be considerable. According to her, cricketing criminality is alive and well here too. But since you have a prior engagement ...'

'Wait just a moment. I don't think Pat would be particularly affronted if you were to deliver this lady along to her unit tomorrow. She could bring us both up to date on this deplorable side of the game while we watch the match in progress. After all, watching cricket and conducting a conversation are not mutually exclusive activities. And as I recall both Pat and her late husband, Albert, were great cricket-lovers. He was a member of the Cricket Ground Trust and he and Pat were regulars in the Members' Stand at most tests and State matches. I'm sure Pat will be as interested as I in hearing what your friend has to say. I'll ring Pat now to check with her, but you can take it as read that if you do not hear from me within the next ten minutes that you and your friend will both be welcome to join Pat and I in front of her TV from ten tomorrow morning.'

'Hodgkiss, I shall look forward to it.'

❊   ❊   ❊

As Hodgkiss anticipated, Pat Strong had no objection to Jan Campbell-Jones and her friend joining them to watch the cricket the following day.

'In fact Jan and this friend of hers are likely to liven proceedings up a little,' Pat had told Hodgkiss when he rang. 'Particularly if the cricket's slow and she's got some interesting gossip to retail. Besides, you're not much company sometimes when you get absorbed in the game.'

The next morning Pat was standing on the balcony of her second floor bedroom when Esme stopped her small beige sedan outside the block of units in an exclusive cul-de-sac in that part of Kylerbrin which local real estate agents referred to as the Golden Triangle.

Hodgkiss climbed out, waved to Pat then made his goodbyes to Esme who tooted the horn once then waved to Pat over the car's roof as she made a neat three-point turn in the narrow street then drove away.

Pat hurried downstairs to the kitchen where she operated the various electronic devices that would allow Hodgkiss to enter the grounds then the building itself.

'Why didn't you ask Esme to come in for a cuppa?' Pat demanded as she held the door open for Hodgkiss.

'Esme didn't want a cuppa,' Hodgkiss replied bluntly. 'But I wouldn't say no.'

Pat shook her head. 'No. You never do. Well, why don't you go and make it yourself? You know where everything is ... or you should by now. What time are Jan and her friend coming?'

'I told Jan to arrive around ten.' He glanced at his watch. 'They should be here any minute now.'

'I think they've just arrived,' said Pat, who had walked through to the lounge and was standing, looking out the front picture window. 'I'll turn on the tele — you let them in when they buzz.'

Hodgkiss operated the necessary buttons and soon Pat and her friend, a well made woman of an age similar to Jan — early forties — were waiting at the front door to Pat's unit.

Hodgkiss pulled the door open and stood to one side. 'Good morning, ladies. Do come in.'

Jan performed the introductions. 'Mary Fraser ... Edgar Hodgkiss.'

Mary smiled broadly and held out a small but competent hand. 'Good morning, Edgar. Jan has mentioned you on the odd occasion. I believe you and your friend Mrs Strong are both cricket lovers.'

'Indeed we are,' said Pat, joining the group.

She led the way through to the front lounge where a large wall-mounted television set showed a high shot of a cricket ground completely surrounded by crowded grandstands.

'Perfect timing,' said Pat. 'The umpires are just coming out.'

Jan and Mary settled in two wide armchairs with deep seats and Pat and Hodgkiss sat cosily side-by-side on a two-seater lounge.

Mary commented: 'I notice you have the sound turned off. Is that how you generally watch the cricket?'

Pat nodded. 'Yes. Hodgkiss can't stand the commentators and I must say I agree with him. Sometimes we listen to the commentary on the radio. It's not always brilliant, but it's usually an improvement on the drivel you usually get from that lot on the tele.'

Mary chuckled. 'You'll get no argument from me about that. Jack, my husband, did exactly the same. He turned the sound off. Always. He couldn't stand it. He used to go ballistic at some of the silly things they said. One of his pet hates was a phrase they nearly always came out with whenever we were struggling to make a winning score: "All Australia needs now is runs", or if the other side looked like winning you'd be sure to hear one of them say, "All Australia needs now is wickets." I mean, how silly can you get.'

'I couldn't agree more,' said Hodgkiss, nodding vigourous agreement. 'It's that kind of vacuous platitude repeated *ad nauseam* that turned me off listening to the TV commentary. That and the re-runs of every second ball; the endless inane analysis and the repetition and dissection of every insignificant detail. They seem to suffer under the delusion that they must fill every second of air time with words, no matter how trite, repetitive or irrelevant.'

Mary nodded agreement. 'Yes, and I know Jack used to

object to the introduction of all the latest technological gimmickry. He thought it spoiled the game.'

'A man after may own heart,' said Hodgkiss. 'Everyone knows that umpires aren't infallible. Sometimes they give wrong decisions. They always have since the game began.'

Mary put in. 'My Jack used to say that getting a bad decision was part of the game. Learning to cope with it was one of the ways a player learned sportsmanship.'

'Then I suspect that your Jack would have been horrified at many aspects of the way the game is played today. For instance, I'll bet he never approved of the way the players run in to the pitch and jump all over each other every time a batsman gets out. I know when I was playing and a wicket fell, there was none of this running around and hugging and thumping each other on the back. Celebrating they call it. When I played years ago when a batsman got out we'd just sit down on the grass and have a rest until the next man came in. Why, it won't be long before they start ripping off their shirts like the footballers and running around the field with their arms spread out like demented aeroplanes.'

'Your right there, Mr Hodgkiss ...'

'Edgar, please.'

'Another thing Jack couldn't stand was seeing a fieldsman with his hands in his pockets.'

Pat nodded towards the screen. 'Looks like they're starting at last.'

And so the four settled down to watch the match.

For the most part they watched in silence with the odd comment and occasional interjections of 'good shot.'

At one point Jan commented, pointing towards the screen: 'Look at that fellow, Hodgkiss, the one fielding at Long On. Hands in pockets! Naughty, naughty!'

'Don't make jokes about it, Jan,' said Hodgkiss stiffly. 'Hands in pockets is not the way to play cricket, even in the outfield like that fellow.'

Minutes later the batsman played a defensive stroke, missed, and the ball flew through to the wicketkeeper. At once there was a confident appeal from all of the fieldsmen which the umpire immediately turned down.

Mary shook her head. 'It's just so silly when they all appeal like that. Take this fellow in the outfield nearest us; he must be thirty metres from the bat. How could he possibly have heard anything even if there *was* a snick. It's just plain silly. Their coach or their manager or someone should tell them to stop making silly appeals and behave themselves.'

Hodgkiss nodded agreement. 'Unfortunately it's become part of the game of bluff. The louder they shout the more the umpire will feel intimidated ... or that's the theory anyway. But of course the umpires aren't fooled. And a damned good thing too.'

The play continued and only minutes later one of the batsmen was clean bowled.

At once the fieldsmen swarmed towards the sturdy dark-haired bowler, surrounding him, hugging him, slapping him on the back, the arms or any other part of his anatomy they could reach in the crush.

Pat observed. 'What's the matter with our friend in the outfield; the hands-in-pockets fieldsman? He hasn't run in like the rest of them.'

'And he's put his hands in his pockets again,' said Jan with mock outrage.

A new batsman hurried to the crease, took guard, looked around the field and the match continued.

A few overs later, with a different bowler, a tall man with

fiery red hair, the ball struck the batsman on the pads. At once there was another loud, confident appeal from all the fieldsmen who immediately began to run towards the centre of the ground, anticipating the celebration of another wicket falling.

Even the fieldsman who had been the subject of their derogatory hands-in-pockets comments ran in from his position in the outfield towards where the bowler stood, frozen, arms outstretched theatrically, legs apart, in a desperate effort to sway the umpire with his display of confidence.

But the umpire appeared quite unmoved. He remained stooped, his attention fixed on the batsman's pads where the ball had struck. Slowly he rose and moved his hands in a square, index fingers extended, indicating that he required the assistance of the 'third umpire.'

The fieldsmen stood quietly in groups, eyes fixed on a television screen set into the massive electronic scoreboard where the fate of the batsman would be displayed.

'That fellow has still got his ruddy hands in his pockets,' said Hodgkiss pointing towards the screen where that outfielder was standing apparently chatting to the bowler.

'Why don't you write a letter to the editor about it if you feel so strongly,' Pat suggested.

'I might do just that.'

Then the words Not Out appeared on the scoreboard screen in huge italic letters.

The two batsmen, who had been chatting apparently nonchalantly in the middle of the pitch, returned to their respective ends, the ball was thrown back to the red-headed bowler, the fieldsmen hurried back to their positions and the match resumed.

'Looks like our chap doesn't approve of the decision,' Jan remarked, pointing to the screen where the outfielder at Long On, having returned about half way to his position, had paused and was digging his heels angrily into the turf.

'I don't see why *he* should be put out by the decision,' said Mary. 'From where he was standing he wouldn't have a clue whether or not the fellow was likely to be out leg before wicket. He's completely in the wrong position to judge.'

'Exactly,' said Hodgkiss. 'It's just part of their bully-boy tactics … not that it does them much good, particularly now the umpires have all these electronic gadgets available to back them up.'

And so the game continued without any great excitement, except for the occasional flurry of scoring, until the players left the field for lunch.

'Well, we might have a bite to eat too,' said Pat, rising. 'I've made some sandwiches. Wait here and I'll fetch them and some coffee.'

Hodgkiss followed Pat out to the kitchen and helped brew fresh coffee and arrange a variety of sandwiches and cakes on two large serving platters.

When they returned Jan and Mary had moved out to the balcony to enjoy the early afternoon sunshine.

By the time they had finished their lunch and Hodgkiss had returned the cups, saucers and plates to the kitchen and stacked them in the dishwasher, the cricketers were returning to the field.

Play continued uneventfully and at a rather slow pace.

At the end of one particularly dull maiden over Hodgkiss turned to Mary: 'Jan mentioned that you have some inside knowledge of certain criminal aspects of the game,' he said with a nod towards the television screen.

Mary nodded. 'Yes, I suppose you could say that. My husband and I always loved the game and both of us played at quite a high level. Unfortunately he passed on unexpectedly to that great pitch in the sky three years ago. At the time he was active in administration at a national level, particularly in efforts to keep the game clean. Now I'm doing my best to continue his work.

'Contrary to what people may think corruption on the cricket field is by no means restricted to the Indian sub-continent. It is a growing problem right here and in most cricket-playing countries.'

Hodgkiss shook his head. 'That's very depressing news. But I suppose where ever there is gambling there is always the potential for corruption.'

'Yes indeed. Unfortunately these days it is possible to lay a bet on most aspects of every sort of sport, not just cricket. Sponsorship of sporting events with all the huge money paid out to the players has a lot to answer for.'

'Oh, I don't think it's altogether fair to blame the sponsors for corruption in sport,' said Jan. 'I mean, the viewers love it or they wouldn't watch.'

'That's true enough,' said Mary, 'but it is the kind of lionization that arises from promotion of sport and so-called sports stars and the huge sums of money paid to these people that has sent the whole concept of sport completely off the rails. It is no longer frowned upon to deliberately inflict serious physical injury upon your opponent in the name of sport. An assault may be committed on the sports field that would anywhere else be the subject of immediate arrest followed by a criminal charge.'

'I wouldn't argue with any of that,' said Hodgkiss, 'but that's getting rather off the subject. Assault is not the sort of criminal behaviour you were talking about, was it?'

Mary smiled grimly. 'Indeed it was not, Edgar, but there is such thing as assault with a cricket ball when the intent is there. What I was referring to was gambling … and murder, and that is not mere speculation. In fact I have credible information that a murder is actually being planned at present.'

'Murder!' Pat and Hodgkiss chorused.

'Who's going to be murdered?' Pat asked.

'And who's going to do the murdering? Hodgkiss demanded.

Mary shook her head slowly. 'I just wish I knew. No one can say who is the target or when they're likely to be killed or how or by whom.'

'That's all very vague and unsatisfactory,' said Hodgkiss. 'Without some sort of detail the idea is hardly credible, is it?'

'Normally I would agree with you, Edgar, except that the information about the threat is coming persistently from some very reliable sources with contacts close to the biggest gambling syndicates — the Indian Connection as it's known locally — and for that reason it would be fool-hardy to ignore the threat. These sources have been right too often in the past to ignore them now.'

'And what do they say? Do they have anything concrete to offer at all?'

'Yes. For what it's worth the word is that there was a big wager placed but that the person who was to deliver on the bet — in this case a fast bowler from this State, so it could be either of the opening bowlers here today — originally agreed to do as he was paid to do but for some reason he has changed his mind and told the bookmakers that he intends to renege on the deal.'

'And do we know the precise terms of this wager?'

'Actually we don't *know* anything, but the word is that the bowler was supposed to bowl a No Ball on the fifth delivery in his first over of the day.'

'Well, neither of the opening bowlers has bowled a no ball at all today, so if the bet was on this match then it may have been one of those two who welshed on the deal, so he could be in the gamblers' bad books right now.'

Mary raised an eyebrow. 'True, but it's not only the professional gamblers who are going to be upset; some of the players are involved in betting too. And there is also the personal angle. Some of our cricketers are bits of lads where the ladies are concerned so there's also the possibility that the murderer could be an irate husbands as well as a vengeful gambler.'

'Oh, so there's a bit of *that* goes on too, is there?' said Jan. 'And here's me thinking it was a game for gentlemen.'

'Some of them are worse than others, of course,' said Mary. 'Now, that fellow bowling now, he's notorious for getting into bed with the wives of other players.'

'You mean that fellow with red hair, the one who had his appeal for leg before wicket turned down a moment ago?'

'That's the fellow. Very popular with the ladies, from all reports.'

Hodgkiss asked: 'And what do you know, if anything, about the fieldsman who puts his hands in his pockets?'

Mary pointed towards the screen. 'Oh, the fellow at Long On, d'you mean? His name's Jason Morrison. He's supposed to be a batsman but his performance this season has been pretty ordinary.'

'And is he part of the gambling scene so far as you know?'

Mary shrugged. 'Who knows who is part of it and who isn't. There is so little that anyone actually knows for certain. If we actually *did* know who was involved and who wasn't you can bet that the authorities would be doing something about it. But so far as I know there's no bad vibes around about Morrison. But that's not to say he's clean.'

'It must be very difficult for the really straight ones to operate in an atmosphere of such suspicion,' Pat observed.

'That's the really hard part about it,' said Mary. 'There's probably only one or two really rotten apples in any of top flight teams, but everyone — all the players — feel as if they're somehow under suspicion. It's so bad for the game.'

The discussion lapsed and the four turned their attention to the play once more in time to see the red-haired bowler take the ball to begin a new over.

On his third ball the batsman scooped up an easy catch which was taken by the fieldsman at cover point.

At once all the players ran in to help the bowler celebrate his triumph.

Hodgkiss pointed at the screen. 'Even the hands-in-pockets fieldsman from Long On, is joining the throng this time.'

Sure enough the player whom Mary had identified as Jason Morrison had run in and joined the group of players surrounding the bowler, giving high fives and delivering hearty slaps on the bowler's back, shoulders and buttocks.

The dismissed batsman left the field, pulling off his batting gloves, head drooping, while the surviving batsman leaned casually on his bat, watching the orgy of congratulation with contempt.

The replacement batsman ran down the steps from the pavilion and began his progress towards the pitch in business-like manner, skipping then stretching by raising his bat over his head with both hands, preparing to do battle.

But the fieldsmen had not yet returned to their positions. Most were still crowded around the bowler who was now talking to the umpire and apparently experiencing some difficulty.

He was doubled over and two of his colleagues were crouched beside him consulting and appearing to offer urgent advice on his condition.

Another group of five or six players was crowded into a circle nearby, heads down, examining something which one of the players was displaying on the palm of an outstretched hand.

Only Morrison had returned to his position in the outfield where he was down on one knee, apparently retying his bootlaces.

Pat reached for the remote. 'I'll turn the sound up and see what's going on there.'

At once the excited voice of one of the commentators broke in.

'And we're just getting a message through now. We've been told that Jim Cameron ..."

'that's the red-headed bowler,' Mary supplied.

' ... has been stung by a wasp ... something like that. One of the players apparently found it clinging to the back of his shirt.'

'Could have been a bee,' offered a second voice, not to be denied a contribution to this dramatic moment in the commentary.

'Or any kind of stinging insect ... perhaps a sand fly,' suggested a third voice eagerly. 'Sand flies can give you a nasty bite too.'

'Yes, that's right ... in fact any kind of stinging insect,' the first commentator stressed, eager to regain control.

He continued, an edge of alarm in his voice. 'Now what's this?! It looks like Jim Cameron's collapsed.'

Sure enough the red-headed bowler was now measuring his length on the ground just beside where the umpire stood.

The second voice offered: 'Perhaps he's had some kind of re-action to the bee sting, or sand fly or whatever it was that stung him.'

'Yes, some people can be very allergic to stings from bees … or wasps … or sand flies or even bed bugs.'

The third voice chimed in. 'It could be a prophylactic reaction. I think that's what it's called when you get a reaction from a bee sting.'

The second voice was not so sure. 'Um. I don't think you've got that quite right, mate. Isn't that something to do with … er, um. … you know … when you go with your girlfriend.'

The first voice moved quickly to save the situation by resuming authoritatively. 'We've just been informed that a stretcher has been called for, so it seems that Cameron might not be in a position to continue in the attack at this point in time.'

Right on cue two men in the uniform of ambulance officers emerged from the gate in front of the main grandstand pushing a wheeled stretcher quickly towards the centre of the ground.

Meanwhile the umpire had detached himself from the scrum of cream-clad players and appeared to be speaking earnestly into a mobile phone, turning to glance back occasionally towards the recumbent, motionless figure on the ground.

'I don't like the look of this,' said Jan.

Moments later the first commentator resumed in hushed tones. 'We have just received the most distressing news, but I must stress that this has not yet been officially confirmed, but we have just been informed from a reliable source that Jim Cameron has passed away within the past few minutes.'

Now the two ambulance officers were crouched over the prone figure apparently making desperate efforts to revive him.

Hodgkiss took a mobile phone from his shirt pocket and punched in a set of numbers. Pat reached for the remote and turned down the sound on the television again.

Hodgkiss spoke earnestly into his phone. 'Donald. Are you at the cricket with Esme and the inspector as you had planned?' He paused briefly. 'You are? Excellent. Are you watching at present or are you perhaps at the bar? Good. Then you cannot have failed to notice that one of the players, the bowler, Jim Cameron — the one with the red hair — has collapsed and very likely is dead, or that is the unofficial view just now passed on by one of the television commentators. If the unfortunate fellow is not dead now you may be sure that very soon he will be. Yes. Yes. Now, will you kindly cease asking inane questions and listen to what I have to say for just one moment without interruption. What you must do now is to take yourself and the inspector immediately to the centre of the ground and assume control of the situation because I have no doubt this will become a murder inquiry.'

For a moment Hodgkiss moved the phone away from his ear, at the same time raising his eyes to the ceiling.

'The fool has hung up.' He dialed again. 'Esme. I have just spoken to Donald and predictably he has behaved quite irrationally … yes, yes. Nevertheless I can assure you that the fellow has undoubtedly been the victim of a murderous attack. Very well. Now, since Donald will not heed my advice in the matter will you kindly hand your phone to Inspector O'Hare. I am confident that he will have no qualms about acting upon my advice. I'm sure that he has not forgotten, as

Donald apparently has, the many occasions upon which my suggestions … Yes, Yes. Very well. I agree.'

Hodgkiss shook his head, disconnected the call and returned the phone to his pocket.

He announced: 'Esme has agreed to pass on my advice directly to the Inspector. I am confident that he will have sufficient nous to take seriously what I had to say and initiate an official investigation without delay.'

Pat protested; 'But Edgar, you had no grounds whatever to think that poor fellow had been murdered. Bee stings can be really serious if the victim isn't treated at once, particularly if the person has a severe allergy of some kind.'

Hodgkiss frowned. 'I have no doubt you're understanding of the medical possibilities are quite correct. Nevertheless, I have good reason to believe that the fellow is the victim of foul play.'

Pat shook her head in dismay. 'But he was stung by a bee or a wasp. Some of the fieldsmen were gathered around in a group looking at it … whatever it was that stung him. One of them had it in his hand. The commentator said they found it clinging to the back of his shirt, didn't he?'

Hodgkiss shrugged. 'I dare say they were looking at something, but whatever it was, it was not what killed that man. The poison that killed him did not originate from an insect, although it is true, as you pointed out, that some insects may cause a fatal anaphylactic reaction if not immediately treated. Believe me, that poor fellow's death was caused by some man-made and man-operated instrument that delivered a swift-acting and very powerful deadly poison.'

Pat prodded Hodgkiss and nodded towards the screen. 'Look! It seems your phone call has got some action.'

On the screen Donald and the imposing, uniformed

presence of Inspector O'Hare were to be seen making their way purposefully towards the centre of the ground, heads together, apparently in animated consultation.

'Taking their ruddy time, aren't they?' Hodgkiss commented sourly. 'While they dawdle no doubt the murderer is covering his tracks.'

'Oh, come off it, Hodgkiss,' said Jan. 'How could the murderer — assuming that a murder was actually committed there, which I seriously doubt — possibly be covering his tracks in full view of about sixty thousand people at the ground and heaven knows how many hundreds of thousands or even millions more people watching on television. He'd have to be a pretty cool customer I'd say.'

Pat turned up the sound on the television again.

One of the commentators observed, 'It seems that the police have decided to take an interest in what's happened here. I wonder what they've been told that makes them think they need to become involved.'

A second voice ventured. 'Yes, and I wonder what they plan to do about it.'

Hodgkiss muttered. 'Don't we all.'

The first voice continued. 'Now the police are in conference with the ambulance men and they seem to be discussing whether or not to remove the ... Jim Cameron.'

Hodgkiss interrupted scornfully. 'How would those idiots know what the police are thinking? Anyway, it's as well that they don't because Donald wouldn't have a sensible thought in his head.' He paused. 'Now, I think the time has come to offer the long arm of the law a little more assistance.'

Again Hodgkiss took the mobile phone from his pocket again and thumbed in a series of numbers.

On the screen the camera had zoomed in on Donald and

the inspector just in time to show Donald reaching into his jacket pocket and taking out a mobile phone.

The picture was close enough to show the look of fury that appeared on Donald's face as soon as he saw the caller's number on the screen of his phone.

He raised the phone to an ear, then catching his own huge image on the scoreboard screen, he turned quickly away.

Hodgkiss began. 'Donald, let me say at once that the advice which I am about to offer is not given lightly and to quote a character from one of your favourite TV programmes, I will say this only once. Naturally you are free to take my advice or ignore it as you have so often in the past, ultimately to your cost. If you feel that you may not be inclined to heed what I say perhaps you should hand your phone to the inspector now, as I feel he may have greater confidence in my suggestions than you.'

Hodgkiss paused, eyes on the television set.

In the middle of the ground Donald stood stock still.

Interpreting silence for consent Hodgkiss pressed on. 'Very well, then. I shall proceed. The first thing to do is to secure the murder weapon ...'

Donald swung sharply through one hundred and eighty degrees and flung up both arms.

Hodgkiss continued. 'Donald, kindly stop leaping around in that uncoordinated manner and pay attention.

Hodgkiss paused and listened briefly. 'Yes. That's what I said "'secure the murder weapon.'" Another short pause.

On the ground the camera obligingly showed Donald head down, speaking aggressively into his mobile phone.

'Yes, Donald, of course I know where it is to be found or I would not be offering to tell you where to find it and, to answer your other question, yes, I could speculate with confidence on the exact nature of the weapon. Do you really think I would be urging you to secure it if I did not know what it is and where it may be found?

'Then, once you have the murderer weapon in your possession the next step will be to secure the evidence that will enable you to undertake a successful prosecution.'

Hodgkiss paused again while on the screen Donald was shown talking in an agitated manner into his mobile phone.

'Yes, Donald. I quite understand that, but if you will kindly show enough confidence in my judgment for just another five minutes I am quite sure that you will then be in a position to continue the investigation to a successful conclusion without any further assistance from me. Does that satisfy you? Excellent.

'Now, if you turn around through ninety degrees you will see about fifty metres in front of you a fieldsman in a position which I believe is known as Long On. Do you see the fellow I mean? I believe his name is Jason Morrison.'

On the screen Donald's head bobbed in exaggerated assent.

'Very well. Now, I want you to approach him, but in such a fashion that there is no suggestion that you are about to apprehend him. In other words, do not alarm him. I do not want to afford him the opportunity to cover his tracks in any way by destroying valuable evidence.'

Hodgkiss paused, listening.

'Yes, of course you are going to arrest him. Why do you think I pointed him out to him? So you could exchange pleasantries. Donald, you should know from your experience over the years that I am not given to the waste of police time and resources, so please do just as I have asked. Walk casually towards the fellow, perhaps with your eyes down as if you are scrutinizing the ground. Then when you are close enough seize him, restrain him and order him to lay on the ground and most important, *he must not put his hands in his pockets.* Is that clear?'

Hodgkiss and the three women, now on the edge of their seats, watched as Donald began a circuitous and cautious advance in the direction of the fieldsman at Long On, pretending to examine the screen of his mobile phone as he progressed. When he was within about three metres of his quarry Donald closed the gap in three quick strides which brought the two men face to face. Then the two appeared to engage in a vigourous debate which ended with the fieldsman shrugging his shoulders, stepping back and lying, face down, full length on the grass, arms extended to both sides.

'Excellent,' said Hodgkiss into his mobile phone. 'Now I want you to examine very closely the turf in the area not far from where that man was standing. What you are looking for is some small sharp metal object that has been pushed down into the ground. It will certainly be a blade of some kind, very likely with the traces of some potent poison still on its tip so when you discover it handle it with the greatest caution.'

He paused, listening, then continued. 'Yes, I agree that the cricket ground is a very large area, however I believe I can guide you to the spot with some certainty. If not to the exact spot, then somewhere very close to where he buried his weapon. Now, turn through ninety degrees and take three steps to your left … stop … turn to your right … forward … stop … a little further … stop. Now, turn to your left again. Forward … a little more. Now stop. I believe you will find it buried very close to where you are standing now.'

Having completed a series of manoeuvres that any casual observer at the ground or viewer on TV may have taken to be a rather slow, poorly choreographed and complicated dance step, Donald stopped, stooped then went down on hands and knees. With nose close to the ground he began a slow, minute examination of the grass.

Jan chuckled. 'He looks like German Short Haired Pointer hard at work.'

Suddenly Donald paused in his scrutiny, reached into a slacks pocket and drew out a bunch of keys. He selected one of the keys and began digging into the turf.

The fieldsman Morrison, who had now risen to a sitting position, appeared to take this digging process as a signal to begin a slow crawl towards the nearest exit from the ground.

Hodgkiss spoke urgently into his phone. 'Donald, might I suggest that you suspend digging, leave your keys on the ground to mark where you have made your discovery and turn your attention to the culprit who appears to be planning to decamp.'

Abruptly Donald looked up, dropped the bunch of keys on the grass then sprang to his feet and walked quickly in the direction of the fieldsman who was now crawling rapidly toward the boundary fence. Donald stood over the man, waving a forbidding finger and apparently issuing instructions. The man lay down again, arms extended as before and Donald returned to where his keys lay on the grass.

Hodgkiss continued. 'Well done, Donald. Now that you appear to have discovered the murder weapon it is time to look for the evidence necessary to secure a conviction.

'This you will find in the right hand pocket of Morrison's cricketing flannels.

'I suggest you take him forthwith to the dressing rooms, caution him and place him under arrest then require him to remove his trousers so that you can take them away for forensic examination. In the meantime do not allow him to do anything that might interfere with the contents of the righthand pocket.

'Thorough testing of the lining of the pocket will, I am confident, reveal traces of the poison which he used to kill Cameron and, if you are lucky, perhaps some evidence of the venomous insect that he used as a diversion to draw attention away from the real instrument of death.'

He added hastily. 'Oh, and one more thing before you go; you must take steps to obtain a full tape of the proceedings of this cricket match because it contains crucial evidence of Morrison's crime.'

Hodgkiss paused, pondering, lips pursed, eyes upturned. 'Yes. I think that's all. Ring me if you have any problems.'

He cut the connection and turned to the others.

'Not a bad day's work, wouldn't you say.'

Open-mouthed, Pat shook her head. 'Hodgkiss, you are the most unbearable, insufferable, most conceited …'

'Conceited!' Hodgkiss exclaimed. 'But, I only …'

'Yes. Conceited: smug, arrogant, vain, self-important. Or don't you know the meaning of the words.'

Hodgkiss sat down heavily on the sofa beside Pat. 'I know what the words mean, but I am having some difficulty applying any of them to my recent behaviour. I think I showed a good deal of patience, restraint and tolerance towards Donald in view of …'

Pat cut him off. 'Patience, restraint and tolerance! Hodgkiss, if only you could have heard yourself. Your patronising tone! Your dismissive attitude! Really, sometimes it's no wonder Donald refuses to listen or even talk to you.'

Hodgkiss shrugged. 'Well, I can only say that it's a good job he agreed to listen to me today.'

'Really, and what makes you so sure you've got it all right?'

'Yes,' said Jan. 'I'd like to know what made you think that Morrison had anything to do with it. And what made you so sure that bowler fellow had been murdered anyway?'

Hodgkiss nodded towards Mary. 'Well, for a start there was what Mary told us only this morning. Correct me if I'm wrong, Mary, but I think you said that the word was out that there may very soon be a murder committed in the local cricketing world and that the victim would be a fast bowler who had reneged on some arrangement he had previously made with a gambling syndicate. In addition you said that the murder could be committed any time; even as soon as today.'

Mary nodded rather uncertainly. 'Well, yes, Edgar, it's true I said all of that. But please remember that's only what I was told. Hearsay, I think you call it. No one knew for certain when or if any of these things would actually happen. Really it was all little more than idle gossip.'

Hodgkiss nodded and continued, unfazed. 'Well, idle gossip or not you seemed fairly confident about it and that was good enough for me. What happened on that field today filled all the conditions of the gossip. There was motive. In fact there were two motives. First there was the gambling aspect and there was also the sexual or shall we say the marital infidelity aspect. Either was on the cards and either would have been strong enough motive in the circumstances.

'But of course there was much more to it than that.

'There was the suspicious behaviour of the fieldsman himself.'

'Really?' said Jan. 'I didn't notice anything particularly suspicious about Morrison's behaviour. In fact I thought it was altogether pretty unremarkable, except for putting his hands in his pockets.'

'Then you weren't really paying attention to him,' said Hodgkiss, waving finger. 'The first thing that drew my attention to him was his conduct whenever a wicket fell or there was an appeal.

'You will have noticed that whenever a batsman was given out all of the players ran in to congratulate the bowler and generally behave in a most juvenile manner.'

'But so did Morrison,' Pat objected. 'If he hadn't he would never have got close enough to the bowler to stab him with whatever it was he stabbed him with … if he actually stabbed him at all.'

Hodgkiss grunted. 'So, you're still not convinced. Very well. Now cast your mind back. The first significant occurrence was the first appeal; an unsuccessful appeal for caught behind. Do you remember that? Everyone except Morrison ran in to congratulate the bowler. This was because the particular fellow who was bowling at the time was not his intended victim — Cameron, the bowler with the red hair.

'There were only two occasions when Morrison ran in to congratulate the bowler. Both times it was when Cameron was bowling. The first time was when an appeal had been made for leg before wicket. As it happened this appeal was turned down so no one, including our man, had the chance to swarm all over the bowler giving him high fives and slapping him on the back and everywhere else.

'But the second time was different. Cameron clean bowled one of the batsmen so there was no doubt about the decision.

'This time Morrison lost no time getting off the mark. He dashed in and was among the first of the crowd of players slapping Cameron on the back. I watched carefully and he definitely slapped Cameron on the back, high up near his right shoulder blade.

'In fact I noticed at that moment Cameron seemed to flinch as if he had particularly felt Morrison's slap. But since it was followed immediately by many more congratulatory slaps on various parts of his anatomy he may have lost track of who had slapped him where and when. In fact probably he wasn't very perturbed at the time since the initial effects of the wound may not have been very painful, possibly little more than a mild sting.

'The fact that one of the other fieldsmen found a wasp, or whatever it was, almost immediately afterwards confirmed my suspicions about what had happened.

'But soon Cameron began to feel the effects of the poison.

'We saw him speaking to the umpire. No doubt he was complaining of feeling unwell.

'Then very soon after that he collapsed.

'Of course everybody's attention was on Cameron and the drama that followed when the ambulance men arrived and tried to revive him.

'While all that was going on did any of you happen to notice what our man Morrison was doing with himself?'

Hodgkiss looked around the ring of blank faces.

'No, I thought not.'

'Well, Hodgkiss, I've no doubt you did and are going to tell us,' said Pat. 'So what was he doing?'

'He had moved away from where the others were gathered and was unobtrusively burying the murder weapon. I saw him down on one knee pretending to tie his shoe laces, but really he was pushing the weapon he had used to kill Cameron into a particular spot of turf which he had previously loosened by digging into it with the heels of his shoes in a display of pretended frustration at an earlier decision going against his team.

'No doubt he had decided it would be wise to dispose of the weapon as soon as possible in case someone should tumble to his deception with the venomous insect and decide that it was necessary to conduct an immediate investigation. This would almost certainly involve searching everyone who had been on the scene at the time Cameron was struck.'

Pat asked. 'And what was it … this weapon Morrison used.'

'Heavens, Pat. I don't know *exactly* what it was. But, as I said to Donald, it would have been some sharp metal object; a blade, a needle perhaps; and small enough to conceal in his pocket with safety and hold in his hand without anyone noticing anything untoward.

'We all noticed that Morrison frequently had his hand in that pocket. No doubt he was anxious to keep the poisoned weapon properly shielded and in a position where it could do *him* no mischief. Perhaps he had a cap over the poisoned tip and was checking frequently to see that it was firmly in place.

'But whatever the nature of the weapon it appears that Donald has found it, so he'll be able to supply all of the details when he arrives home tonight.'

Jan asked: 'And you think that Morrison left the bee or wasp or whatever it was on the back of the fellow's shirt at the same time that he stabbed him with the … what ever it was he used.'

Hodgkiss nodded. 'No doubt about it. Remember, it was discovered almost immediately after Morrison had slapped Cameron on the back. Then he hurried away to bury the implement in the piece of ground which he had already disturbed and softened up.

'It would have been simple enough for him to stab Cameron and in the same motion crush the insect — which was no doubt already dead — against his shirt so that it would stick there even if only for a moment or two. It would be certain that someone would notice it when Cameron complained of being stung on that spot. Even if it fell off his shirt and onto the ground someone would more than likely see it and even if they didn't Morrison could have drawn attention to it.'

Pat shook her head. 'Hodgkiss, I still think there was an awful lot of guess work in all of that.'

Hodgkiss frowned. 'Guess work! I don't think I'd call it guess work, Pat. Imaginative reconstruction would be a more accurate and fairer description of my contribution.'

'Very imaginative indeed,' Pat confirmed. 'Now, let's see what's happening out there now. I'll turn the sound back up.'

During this discussion all four had managed to divide their attention between the conversation and events on the cricket field where Donald apparently had extracted some object from the turf, placed it in a plastic bag taken from a trousers pocket, then escorted a submissive Morrison from the playing field.

Pat reached forward, thumbed the remote and immediately the commentators voice announced that the game had been abandoned.

'We understand from one of our sources in the dressing room that the police have asked match officials to abandon the game while they continue to investigate this ...,' he paused for effect ... 'very mysterious death.'

A second voice chimed in. 'We haven't yet been able to get an explanation for the actions of the plainclothes officer ... the chap who had been paying a lot of attention to one of the fieldsman, Jason Morrison. Viewers will recall that this officer spoke briefly to Morrison who then lay on the ground and remained there for some time. The officer dug around in the grass nearby then escorted Morrison from the field.

There is nothing to say that Morrison was actually under arrest but the plain clothes policeman was certainly sticking very close to him.

A second voice chimed in. 'And I wonder what that copper was doing prodding around in the ground out near Long On. It looked like he actually dug something up, wouldn't you say?'

'Yeah!' one of the others confirmed. 'And he put it in his pocket, too.'

'Yeah!' said a fourth voice. 'Yeah! He put it in a plastic bag first then into his pocket. That was pretty weird. I mean, it'd make you think that that guy, whoever he was — I suppose he'd be a detective, right? — thought that Morrison might've had something to do with … with what happened.'

'Yeah! We're still trying to get confirmation on that, but no one's saying anything officially at the moment.'

Hodgkiss exploded. 'Oh, for heaven's sake turn the idiots off.'

But before Pat could turn off the set the first commentator resumed, reporting in agitated tones. 'Wait a moment. We've just had a report from one of the game officials in the dressing room. It appears that the detective who escorted Morrison off the field has just left the ground, presumably to return to his police station, but he has taken with him Morrison's cricketing creams; has shirt and trousers.'

'His creams!' exclaimed the second voice. 'Whatever for?'

Pat thumbed the control and the television screen went mercifully blank.

'Well, Donald is certainly not letting the grass grow under his feet,' Jan observed. 'I suppose you'll want to be getting home to ambush him to have all of your grisly speculation confirmed.'

Hodgkiss nodded. 'I think all of us would like to have our

fears confirmed as soon as possible, wouldn't we? I'm sure Mary, as a person with a serious interest in keeping the game clean, would be as keen as anyone, to know the truth. After all, murder at the wicket is a rather novel and dramatic event.'

Jan rose and reached for her handbag.

Pat sighed. 'It's OK, Jan. I'll drive him home. He won't be happy until he's wrung every last detail out of Donald. Sorry our afternoon has been derailed in this way.'

'Not half as sorry as poor Jim Cameron,' said Mary. 'He was such a nice fellow. Really charming. All the cricketing wives and girlfriends really loved him.'

*   *   *

It was just after midnight when Donald turned the unmarked police car into the driveway, Inspector O'Hare seated beside him.

'Are you quite sure it's OK for me to come in,' the inspector asked in a half-whisper. 'I don't want to wake up the whole household.'

Donald grunted as he jerked on the handbrake. 'Don't worry your head about that, boss. Esme always wakes up the minute I set foot in the house no matter what time it is or how quiet I am. And no way will Dad have put his head on the pillow until he's heard every last detail of what we've been up to.'

Donald's prediction proved correct.

When they entered the kitchen through the laundry, Hodgkiss, dressed in pyjamas and a tartan dressing gown that had seen much better days, was waiting with the kettle boiling and Esme had just appeared at the door from the hallway with a pink chenille gown pulled over her nightie.

Three times during the afternoon Donald had declined to take calls from Hodgkiss and Hodgkiss was not in a forgiving mood.

To show his displeasure he turned his back on Donald and greeted the Inspector effusively.

'Inspector O'Hare, wonderful to see you again. And may I congratulate you on a job well done today. Cup of tea?'

'I'd love a cuppa thanks, Edgar,' the inspector replied. 'And as for today's business, well, I don't think we'd have made anything out of it at all but for your help. That was pretty smart considering you worked it out just from watching it all on the tele.'

Hodgkiss shook his head. 'Much as I would like to take full credit I have to admit that there's a good deal more to it than that. I had more than a little help from a lady who's husband was a proficient cricketer in his day and who is herself well up in the business of cricket administration. It was things that she told me that put me on the lookout for foul play before it even happened. Donald should be sure to take a statement from her. I can help put him in contact with her through my friend, Jan Campbell-Jones, if he's interested.'

'We'd really appreciate that, Edgar,' said the inspector, taking a cup of tea from Hodgkiss and sliding his bulk into one side of the narrow built-in pine breakfast nook. 'Now, I suppose you want to hear all about what we've done this evening.'

'If you wouldn't mind,' said Hodgkiss sliding into the seat opposite the inspector.

The Inspector took a gulp of tea and began. 'Well, actually, Edgar, I don't think there's really a great deal we can tell you that you don't already know.'

Donald who had been leaning, grim-faced with his back

to the sink interjected: 'Then why bother to tell him since he knows it all … as usual.'

Hodgkiss ignored the interruption. 'Have you charged the fellow yet … what's his name: Morrison.'

'Oh yes, we've charged him all right,' said the inspector. 'He hasn't signed a confession yet but he's as good as admitted to it. We've got him dead to rights and he knows it. There were stains inside that pocket in his creams that looked pretty suspicious to me. The pants are away being analysed now.

'But what really convinced me you were right is what we found when we turned the pocket inside out. First of all there was a little plastic sheath that he used to cover the poisoned end of the blade that he stabbed the fellow with and also we found in the same pocket a tiny little leg from an insect. Then the insect we recovered from one of the fieldsmen — the one they reckon fell of the bowler's back just before he collapsed — had just the same sort of little leg missing.'

'That's not really proof, though, is it?' said Donald, anxious to minimize his father-in-laws triumph. 'I mean there're a thousand different kinds of insects all over that cricket ground.'

Hodgkiss ignored the interruption. 'What about the blade Donald found buried in the grass not far from where Morrison stood when he was fielding. Was it big enough to take a set of his fingerprints?.'

The Inspector nodded vigourously. 'Yes. His prints were all over it. Forensics are analyzing it for poison at the moment, but there's every sign that it was contaminated on the tip with something or other. Then there's the video of the match. You can actually see Morrison pushing that little blade down into the ground at exactly the spot you guided Donald to.'

Hodgkiss asked. 'Does the video show Morrison preparing

to decamp as soon as he saw Donald start digging for his weapon?'

The inspector nodded enthusiastically. 'Yes. That's another thing that made him look guilty as hell. When Donald stopped him he reckoned that he just wanted to go to the toilet but that's pretty thin. And you'll never guess where Morrison got the idea to use that dead wasp as a diversion?'

Donald groaned aloud but said nothing.

Hodgkiss smiled broadly. 'Oh, I think I can,' he said, turning to Donald who was now looking out the kitchen window into the dark back garden.

Hodgkiss continued. 'By a strange co-incidence Donald and I were discussing only yesterday morning the nature of the plots used in crime fiction.

'As you can imagine, inspector, Donald was of the view that many of these stories are highly improbable and on occasions I would have to agree with him. But this time I suspect that the criminal lifted his *modus operandi* holus-bolus from a detective story. Am I right?'

'You're spot on Edgar,' said the inspector. 'Morrison admitted that he got the idea from an old crime novel. I think it was called *Murder in the Sky* or something like that. Have you read it?'

'It was called *Death in the Clouds*, actually and yes, I have read it, inspector. And quite recently too.'

'Then why don't you lend it to Donald. I reckon he'd be really interested. After all, you never know when another crime might crop up where the criminal gets his idea from a mystery novel.'

Esme, who had been listening to this discussion with mounting concern, decided it was time to intervene.

'Donald's not a great one for reading novels, inspector: are you, Donald. Particularly crime novels. He thinks he gets enough of crime in real life. Would you like another cuppa, inspector?'

Inspector O'Hare shook his head. 'No thanks, Esme. Besides, I think it's time I let you get back to bed. I'll take the car, Donald, and call for you in the morning. OK?'

'Fine with me, boss. I'll see you to the car.'

When they were alone in the kitchen Esme turned to her father, hands on hips.

'Now, Dad, I don't want any grandstanding from you. Understood?'

'Me! Grandstand!' Hodgkiss exclaimed, open mouthed. 'Esme, I've never once …'

But Esme cut him off sharply. 'Oh yes you have, Dad. If you're still here when Donald comes back inside you'll both start talking about what happened out there today and sure as God made little apples it will end up with the pair of you at each other's throats.

'Now, finish your tea, put your mug in the dishwasher and I want you safely tucked up in bed with your light out before Donald comes back inside.'

Unwillingly Hodgkiss complied

Hodgkiss and the Poison Pen

'**H**odgkiss, how would you like a little break … a few days in the country?'

With her tiny phone pressed to an ear, Pat Strong was stretched out on the sunbed on the balcony off the master bedroom in her townhouse located in a short cul-de-sac, regarded as one of the best streets in Kylerbrin.

Seated in the captain's chair at his desk in the front room of the Lillimoor bungalow which he shared with his daughter and son-in-law, Edgar Hodgkiss pursed his lips and frowned.

'Pat, you know what I think of the country; full of nasty things and nowhere interesting to go and nothing interesting to see or do.'

Pat shook her head. 'Not this time, Hodgkiss. I think I could promise you a rather diverting excursion, that is if you are willing to risk it.'

Hodgkiss snorted. 'Now you are trying to make it sound

like a challenge. So what's this diversion? Who, when, what and where?'

Pat replied. 'The who is my cousin Vera. The when is ASAP ... preferably tomorrow first thing. The what is a rather nasty little mystery and the where is Narralong.'

'Narralong? Never heard of the place.'

'Nor had I until Cousin Vera took it into her head to go bush after Roger, her husband, died. Now she's become very attached to the little place.'

'And this "rather nasty little mystery" you mentioned. What does that involve?'

'I think that is best explained in the email Vera sent me this morning. I've forwarded it to you. Read it then ring me back ... with an answer. OK?'

Hodgkiss cut the connection and booted up the computer on his desk. He opened his email and clicked on the message Pat had forwarded.

It read —

Dear Pat,

First I have to apologise for bothering you about this. It must seem an awful cheek since I haven't been in touch with you for so long. But things here look like getting rather out of hand although everyone is trying to ignore it. Quite frankly I think it's time someone did something about it and since no one else seems likely to do it I thought I'd better try.

Do you remember a while back you mentioned that you'd met an old fellow who you told me was really good at solving problems ... problems of a criminal kind since his daughter had married a policeman, a detective I think you said, and this old guy is really smart at solving the crimes while his son-in-law is something of a duffer and would get nowhere but for this old fellow's help.

Well we need some help and I think this old fellow you know might be just the ticket ... if you can persuade him to come. You seem to be thick as thieves with him so please do try. Otherwise I'm concerned that things here could get pretty nasty.

There's been one death already. It was put down to accidental causes or misadventure or something, but everyone knows the poor fellow killed himself. They hush that part of it up because the parish priest we're stuck with at present won't bury suicides in the local cemetery which is a mile or two out of town, so someone persuaded the coroner, who's a local JP, not to bring in suicide although that's obviously what happened.

It probably wasn't too hard to persuade him not to bring in a verdict of suicide because the police never found a suicide note in his house, but the general theory is that someone took it away as well as the nasty letter that the poor man must have received shortly before he died, which probably was why he did what he did, which was an overdose accompanied by lots of whisky.

I expect we'll never really know what happened and why. The poor fellow's funeral is tomorrow or the next day.

I do hope you can come and persuade this criminal mastermind of yours to come with you. If he won't, then you come anyway and perhaps between the two of us we'll be able to muddle through and sort it all out somehow.

Love Vera.

Hodgkiss read the message through a second time then picked up his phone, called down a menu and dialed.

'Well, Hodgkiss, what do you say?' Pat asked, expecting a refusal.

'God knows what you told the woman but she seems to have formed the opinion that I must be approaching senility. It's a wonder she didn't refer to me as an old codger.'

'Neither of us is in the first flush of youth, Hodgkiss. We must learn to live with it. Well, do you want to help or not?'

'Well, nothing very interesting is happening here so I suppose I might just as well go along for the ride.'

'Excellent,' said Pat. 'I'll pick you up first thing tomorrow. Say eight?'

'Very well,' Hodgkiss said, without enthusiasm. 'How long will we be away do you think? I'll have to give Esme some idea.'

'We'll be away for as long as it takes you to sort out their problem, Hodgkiss. How long's a ball of string?'

'I'll tell her a week. That should cover it,' Hodgkiss said, and cut the connection.

He pushed back from his desk and headed down the hall to the kitchen where his daughter, Esme Burke, was preparing their afternoon tea.

*   *   *

At eight the following morning Hodgkiss was waiting on the nature strip outside the Burke's bungalow in a backstreet of East Lillimoor.

In one hand he held a silver thermos of black coffee and in the other a large brown paper bag folded over, containing cream biscuits and four cheese and tomato sandwiches which Esme had made the previous evening and wrapped in greaseproof paper and two pottery mugs.

An overnight bag which he had packed under Esme's supervision, rested at his feet.

Hodgkiss glanced to his right in time to see Pat's top-of-the-range silver Mercedes turn into the street and approach slowly.

When the car stopped Hodgkiss pulled open the rear door, tossed in the bag, then climbed into the front.

'All ready for your challenge, are you, Hodgkiss?' Pat asked, determined to keep the atmosphere light.

'At least poison pen letters are something of a novelty,' Hodgkiss commented. 'So far as I recall I've never had to deal with a poison pen artist before. I don't see why it should present an insurmountable challenge.'

'Well the local police don't seem to have been doing much about it. I would have thought that one man taking his own life would have been enough to get the local bobbies off their tails.'

Hodgkiss shrugged. 'There's not a lot the police can do if the victims aren't putting their hands up for help and reading between the lines of your friend Vera's letter everyone seems to be doing their best to pretend that nothing's happening.'

Pat nodded. 'Yes, I'm afraid you're right there, Hodgkiss. And before we go any further, thank you for agreeing to come. I'd half expected you to refuse. After all you don't know anything about Cousin Vera so there's no reason why you should put yourself out to help solve her problems.'

'But of course they're not just her problems, are they?' said Hodgkiss. 'Again reading between the lines I'd say the problem is sufficiently wide-spread in the community to demand proper attention.'

'So I'm being asked to believe, am I, that your agreement to help is motivated purely by altruism?' Pat asked. 'Somehow

I doubt that. There must be another agenda at work here, particularly bearing in mind your well-known dislike of rural areas: nowhere interesting to go and nothing interesting to do, I think was your summation.'

'Yes, and that is my considered view, generally speaking. However, since you demand an explanation I'll give it to you.'

'Would it have anything to do with Donald being assigned to administrative duties?' Pat asked.

Donald Burke was Hodgkiss' son-in-law, a detective inspector of police stationed at Crestwood, near Lillimoor on Sydney's North Side.

Hodgkiss nodded. 'I won't deny that might have had something to do with it. In fact it is now nearly one month since Donald was re-assigned to administration and consequently there is now almost no chance of an interesting investigation being handed to him consequently no chance of me being able to exercise what Hercule Poirot was pleased to refer to as the little grey cells. Now, having made that confession perhaps you can tell me a little about your Cousin Vera and this Narralong place.'

'Well, there's not a lot to tell about either. As she said in her email, we haven't had a lot to do with each other in recent times. She is the daughter or my late husband Albert's sister. She was married to Roger, a dapper little fellow who was quite a successful suburban solicitor who mostly did rather mundane things like conveyancing and making wills. He died rather suddenly and left Vera quite well off. Since she'd been brought up on a farm she had a sort of residual hankering for the rural life and soon after Roger died she sold the family home, the kids, two boys had long flown the coop, and bought this place in Narralong.'

'Narralong,' said Hodgkiss. 'I'd never heard of it and have

no idea where it is or how long it will take us to get there. Will we need to stop overnight somewhere?'

'Goodness no. It's not that far. Four hours at most.

'Well I'm pleased to hear that. Is it a one- or two-horse town?'

'Only one horse I'm afraid, Hodgkiss. Although it's many many years since I visited Vera. It must be fifteen years at least, but I'd say that it's most unlikely the place would have changed very much in the meantime. Just a railway station and a main street with a clutter of shops and things. A hotel of course, a fish and chip shop and some stock and station agents … or there were then.'

'Does nothing to enhance my picture of rural life,' Hodgkiss muttered, looking dismally through the windscreen.

They stopped briefly at a small, quiet park on the outskirts of one of the villages near the top of the Blue Mountains, did justice to Esme's cut lunch of sandwiches, biscuits and coffee, then got on their way.

'It isn't far now,' said Pat as she steered the big car along a narrow two-lane road running beside a railway line which, from the lack of any traffic, might have been disused.

Then in the distance they both noticed a remarkable procession approaching.

At its head were two large black horses, their wide leather collars decorated by two tall black plumes. The horses were driven by a man, dressed all in black, who sat on the seat of an ancient hearse with high wooden wheels.

A second man, also dressed entirely in black, sat beside him.

Behind the hearse short procession of cars followed, their headlights on.

Pat slowed, pulled the car onto the dirt shoulder, stopped and turned off the motor.

They both watched with interest as the cortege approached.

The driver of the hearse and his companion did not offer even a sideways glance as they passed opposite the parked vehicle.

'A rather striking way to go on your last journey,' Pat remarked. 'I wonder if any of the undertakers in town could turn out a couple of horses like those.'

'Not many stables around our way where you could keep the animals,' Hodgkiss muttered absently, for his attention had been caught by the sole occupant in the last vehicle in the cortege, a small dark sedan.

As the car drew level with the Mercedes the driver, a woman who Hodgkiss put in her late thirties, turned and looked straight at him.

She was not beautiful but certainly striking. She had put back the black veil from her face, probably so she could see the road clearly. Blonde hair showed under the veil.

'What are you looking at, Hodgkiss?' Pat asked, following his glance. 'Or need I ask.'

'I wonder what relation she was to the deceased?' Hodgkiss said.

Pat shrugged as she turned on the motor, put the car into gear and trod gently on the accelerator. 'No doubt Vera will be able to tell you.'

*　　*　　*

The road took a ninety degree bend to the left opposite the Narrolong Railway Station, straightened and continued for three hundred metres. A variety of shops crowded together in this section of road before another right angle bend, this time to the right, took travellers out of town and on their way to the bigger centres to the north and west.

As they drove slowly up the short main street Hodgkiss commented. 'Too many empty shops. Never a good sign.'

Pat glanced out her side window. 'There are quite a few empty shops in the Lillimoor Village these days, Hodgkiss,' she said, then added. 'Sign of the times I'm afraid.'

Instead of turning right at the end of the shops Pat drove straight ahead onto a dirt road that led steeply uphill.

The road ended at the top of the hill at an ancient war memorial where a second dirt road took off to the left.

Pat swung the big car to the left and proceeded at snail's pace.

'This cousin of yours really lives in the boondocks,' Hodgkiss commented as the car bumped down the unmade surface.

He scanned the numbers of the houses as Pat drove.

'It's not much of a road,' he said, 'but the houses are rather fine … for the town.'

Pat commented without taking her eyes off the road. 'Anyone who knows anything about country towns knows that you'll always find the best houses on the highest ground.'

'For the view, I suppose,' said Hodgkiss.

'Yes, for the view of course, and also to be away from the floods.'

Hodgkiss was surprised. 'Floods. Here. I didn't even see a river as we came along.'

'No, you wouldn't have seen it, but there's a creek the other side of the railway line and it's been over the railway station and half way up the main street on more than one occasion.'

Hodgkiss pointed out the side window. 'There it is. Number eight. I'd say it's all right to drive in. There's plenty of room. It looks like quite a large house.'

'Yes, her husband left her very comfortably off,' said Pat as she edged the car down the rutted driveway towards the wide, brick single storey house.

'And that, I take it, is your cousin Vera.'

A large woman of about sixty with a mop of silver hair had appeared at the front door of the house, hands on hips and offering a broad, welcoming smile.

'That's Vera,' said Pat. 'Hasn't changed much in years.'

Pat parked the car in a carport beside the house and they both climbed out.

Hodgkiss took Pat's suitcases from the boot, his bag from the back seat and followed Pat and Vera into the house.

When the introductions were over Vera said: 'I've put you both in the front bedroom. You can have two rooms if you like, but I thought ...'

'The front bedroom will suit very well,' said Pat.

'Fine,' said Vera. 'Well, unpack your things then come along to the kitchen. I suppose you're both dying for a cuppa.'

Five minutes later the three were seated at a long pine table with an enamel top, somewhat chipped at the edges.

Hodgkiss was delighted to see a plate of scones in the centre of the table and beside them a large aluminium teapot with red Bakelite handles, the twin of the one in everyday use in the Burke household.

When the small talk, inquiry about common relations, was out of the way Pat asked: 'Any further developments with your ... problem.'

Before Vera could reply Hodgkiss said. 'As we were coming into town we saw a funeral procession. Would that have been the fellow you think took his own life?'

Vera nodded. 'Yes. That was Mr May ... Arthur. Poor fellow.'

Pat said. 'I think Hodgkiss was more interested in the rather decorative woman in the last of the cars in the procession. A blonde.'

'That would have been Edwina. The schoolteacher, Edwina Foster. She and Arthur were … romantically linked, I think is the way to put it.'

'Lovers, you mean,' said Hodgkiss.

'So the stories go. He was still married, you know, so they were very discreet about it.'

'And did Mr May's wife know about this romantic link?'

Vera shook her head emphatically. 'No. She couldn't have. Poor thing's been in a nursing home for the past two years. Doesn't know what's happening around her any more. Tragic really. She used to be the life of every party and believe it or not Mr Hodgkiss we do have the odd party or two around here still.'

'I'm sure you do, Vera,' said Hodgkiss. 'And please the name's Edgar. When people call me Mr Hodgkiss I'm still inclined to look around to see if my father's made a surprise appearance somewhere.'

'Very well, Edgar. I'm sure poor old Mrs May couldn't have known or cared what Arthur was doing. But of course the town has it's fair share of the self-righteous who tend to see nastiness where there's really nothing but … well, the sort of normal things normal people sometimes get up to.'

Hodgkiss nodded. 'Which brings us to these letters.'

'Yes, I suppose it does,' said Vera, looking across the table at him. 'I suppose you want to hear all about them … what they're about.'

'Do you mean they have a common theme?'

'Oh yes, most certainly. Trees. Whether they should be lopped or not.'

'Really,' said Hodgkiss, surprised. 'Now that's a problem

that often rears it's head in the leafy suburbs around where Pat and I live. I must say I'm a little surprised that it should be such a burning issue out here in the bush. I would have thought you had more than enough trees out here to go around without people making a fuss about them.'

'Well, believe it or not, Edgar. That's our biggest problem in Narrolong. Walk down the street. Ask anyone. They'll tell you the same thing.'

'I don't doubt you for a moment. I know very well how high emotions can run over the question of to lop or not to lop. In the area Pat and I live the council has it's tree preservation policy which is very strict and strictly adhered to. The officer in charge of enforcing the code is referred to as the Tree Nazi. The general consensus is if you want to lop a tree in your own back yard you as well forget it. And of course if you actually want to remove a tree ... well ... it doesn't happen.'

'Sounds like what goes on around here,' said Vera.

'And is the late Mr May's demise somehow related to issues arboreal?'

'"Issues arboreal" Vera repeated. 'I've never heard that one before, but yes, the general view is that the letter which seemed to tip poor old Arthur over the edge was related to his stance on tree lopping. But I have my doubts.'

'And was he pro or anti?'

'Pro ... most emphatically. I've heard him say more than once that big gum trees have no place in people's back yards. They should be in forests.'

'Sounds like a very sensible man,' said Hodgkiss. 'And the letter he received, you mentioned in your email that it appeared to have been removed before he was found. I don't suppose it has come to light since, has it?'

'No and I don't expect it will now. But there might not have been any direct reference in it to trees at all. I think it's far more likely that whoever wrote it wouldn't have bothered to talk about trees. They'd more than likely have made some threat to expose his association with Edwina Foster, which was an open secret in Narrolong.'

Hodgkiss nodded. 'Yes, but do you think perhaps the letter would never have been written if Mr May had been in the anti-lopping camp?'

'Very likely not. If he'd been an anti-lopper they probably would have left him alone. Or that's what I think anyway, although I could be wrong.'

'And how many other letters have there been, have you any idea, Vera?'

Vera wrinkled her nose in doubt. 'It's hard to say, Edgar. I know of four people for sure and they've told me that they think there's been others, but because no one's bothered to go to the police it's hard to say. But I'd say at a guess that it's between six and ten.'

'And the tree business has been the impetus behind them?'

'No doubt, although in one case a lady who I know is heartily against lopping had a letter telling her something unpleasant about her daughter.'

'And was that something unpleasant true or not?'

Vera thought for a moment before answering. 'Probably true, but there'd been stories about the girl doing the rounds for ages before then so it wouldn't have been news to the girl's parents. It was just malicious.'

Hodgkiss nodded. 'These sorts of letters usually are. And have you had one of these unwelcome epistles?'

Very chuckled. 'Oh yes. I had one about a month ago.'

Hodgkiss held up a hand. 'I don't want to see it, but can

you tell me, was it directly related to the tree debate or did it come from some other angle?'

'Trees didn't get a mention. The writer suggested that my fortunate financial situation was founded on my late husband's legal malpractices.'

'So she knew a little of your background then?'

'Apparently … and I notice that you've assumed that the letter-writer is a woman.'

'Yes. So I have. I understand that this is most often the case when these sorts of outbreaks occur … rare as they are, thank goodness. And were you one of the first to receive one of these letters?'

'It's hard to say, but I'm pretty sure there were others before me. I can't really tell you when it started. People have only begun talking about it openly in the last little while.'

'Before Mr May's death, would you say?'

'Oh yes. Certainly before then.'

'And the letters themselves? Do they come through the post? Are they hand delivered? Hand written, printed, pasted up from magazines? What?'

'Well I can only speak for mine but it was typed and on a very old machine, I'd say.'

'And what about the others. Have you heard anything about them?'

'I know at least two others were typed the same as mine.'

'The letters or the envelopes or both?'

'Both in my case, but I don't know about the others, although I'd say it's most likely that if the envelopes were typed the letters would be too, wouldn't you say?'

Hodgkiss nodded. 'Yes. More than likely.'

Vera held up a hand and nodded towards the window. 'I'm afraid we are about to have a visitor. News of your arrival must have hit town already.'

Hodgkiss turned to see an elderly woman hurrying down the drive towards the front door.

He turned to Vera. 'And she is …?'

'Martha Meadows. One of the most active of the anti-lopping faction. So mind your Ps and Qs you two. She was here the day before yesterday and could hardly wait to tell me that the local policeman had just had a letter. He's another pro-lopper of course. Martha teaches something at the local school.'

Vera rose and hurried into the hall as the door bell sounded. Pat and Hodgkiss heard the sound of muffled greetings at the door then footsteps on the bare boards in the hallway.

'So this is the Mr Hodgkiss we've heard so much about,' said Mrs Meadows, smiling archly.

Vera hastened to explain. 'I told Martha that you and Pat had decided to pay us a visit after I told you about our … little problem.'

'And that you are something of a detective, Mr Hodgkiss,' said Mrs Meadows, increasing the voltage of her smile. 'We do hope that you will be able to sort this nasty business out for us because the police don't seem to be doing a thing about it.'

'As I understand it,' said Hodgkiss, 'the people who have been receiving the unsolicited mail haven't so far taken the police into their confidence.'

'And why bother,' Mrs Meadows went on. 'What do you think the police would do. That sergeant fellow, we all know which side of the fence he sits.'

'"Which side of the fence", Hodgkiss echoed feigning surprise. 'I don't quite follow you there, Mrs Meadows. What fence are we talking about here?'

'Oh come come, Mr Hodgkiss. I'm sure you understand. What I'm saying is that Sergeant Flack is well known to be one of those who would tear down every tree in town given the opportunity … and his wife's very much of the same mind. There'd be no point in asking him to investigate who's sending the nasty letters because he'd probably finish up having to arrest one of his friends.'

Hodgkiss nodded. 'Then you think the writer of these nasty little notes is someone in the pro-lopping faction.'

'Well, I wouldn't go that far, Mr Hodgkiss. No one can say for certain because no one knows just how many letters there's been or who received them. People just aren't talking about it much.'

'And have you received one of these unwelcome letters?' Hodgkiss asked innocently.

Yes, I'm afraid I have. And a horrid experience it was too.'

'And what exactly did it say … that is if you don't mind telling us.'

Mrs Meadows lowered her eyes. 'I'd much rather not discuss it, Mr Hodgkiss, unless you insist of course which you are entitled to do since you are here to investigate the matter.'

Hodgkiss shook his head. 'Mrs Meadows, please understand, I am not here to investigate anything. Vera here mentioned to her cousin that these unfortunate letters were being written and received and because of her obvious concern at the situation we offered to come up as moral support. Nothing more,' Hodgkiss lied.

'Well I'm very disappointed to hear that, I'm sure,' said Mrs Meadows. 'There are those of us who thought you were coming up to put an end to the matter. After all, we heard that you had the reputation of being something of a detective.'

Pat decided it was time to have her say. 'It is true that

Mr Hodgkiss has been of assistance to his son-in-law who is a detective. Perhaps that's how this misunderstanding arose.'

'Well, if Mr Hodgkiss has helped his son-in-law he should have a few clues about how to conduct a proper investigation, shouldn't he?'

'That's quite true, Mrs Meadows,' said Hodgkiss, 'and I shall certainly do what I can to help. Now, I understand that you may not wish to discuss the contents of your letter, but perhaps you could tell me whether or not it was delivered through the post, perhaps hand delivered; was it printed, typed, hand-written … what?'

'Oh it definitely came through the post. I saw Phillip the postman put it in my letterbox although of course I had no idea at the time that it was one of *those* letters.'

'And was it printed, or was it put together from an old book or magazine?'

'Oh no. It was definitely typewritten and on an old-fashioned typewriter too, I'd say.'

'And from what you've heard would you say that that's the way most of these letters have been written … on an old typewriter.'

"That's what I've heard from some of people who've had them.'

'And would you mind telling me who these people are?'

'Oh no, Mr Hodgkiss. I couldn't possibly tell you that. I was told this in complete confidence. I can't go around giving out information like that. People would never trust me with a confidence again.'

Hodgkiss heaved an obvious sigh. 'Mrs Meadows, if I am to be in a position where I can be of use in this matter I must have some basic information to work with. Surely you can give me one or two names of people who've had letters so I can begin to gather some data.'

'Well, you could speak to that schoolteacher woman Edwina Foster. I understand she's had a letter.'

'And which camp would she be in. Is she a lopper?'

'Oh heavens yes. She'd cut down every tree in the town given the chance.'

Vera was not about to let this pass. 'Oh come on, now, Martha. That's a bit rough. I've never heard Edwina say a word one way or another on the matter.'

'Well that boyfriend of hers … we all know where he stands … stood,' said Mrs Meadows, hastily correcting himself.

'Mr May, you mean?' said Hodgkiss.

'Yes, Mr May. And I suppose you know she had the cheek to go to his funeral.'

'Cheek?!' said Hodgkiss.

'Yes, cheek. A very thoughtless and heartless act,' Mrs Meadows insisted.

'"Thoughtless … heartless?", Hodgkiss repeated. 'Why on earth do you say that?'

'Because of his wife, of course. The hussy actually drove out to the cemetery at the back of the cortege. What if someone saw her and told his poor wife. Everyone's been able to keep it from her so far but people *will talk* and her making a display of herself going to his funeral like that … well, people can put two and two together.'

'Yes, and come up with five,' said Vera. 'Poor Mrs May is long past caring or knowing about anything that goes on around here. She's been like that for years. You can hardly blame poor old Arthur for taking an interest in a nice young thing like Edwina.'

'She's not all that young. Anyway, I've heard from people

I know at that nursing home that Evelyn May is very lucid from time to time. It would be a tragedy if anyone happened to mention that her husband and that woman were … well … involved.'

'It would be a real tragedy,' Vera said. 'But I'm sure there'd be no one cruel enough to tell her, even if there was anything in it.'

Mrs Meadows smiled knowingly. 'Come along, Vera. There's no need to play the innocent. You know as well as anybody what's been going on there.'

Hodgkiss decided to take a hand. 'If we might return to the matter in hand; the identity of those who have received these letters.' He turned to confront Mrs Meadows. 'Is there perhaps at least one name you can give me?'

Mrs Meadows thought for a moment. 'I understand that sergeant Flack has received one. Quite recently.'

'And who told you that, might I ask?'

'You might ask, Mr Hodgkiss, but I might not tell you. Shall we just say that there are very few secrets in Narrolong.'

'But how can you be so sure of your facts? This is just gossip, surely.'

An unpleasant smirk of triumph suffused Mrs Meadows' face. 'I think not, Mr Hodgkiss. Anyway, perhaps I will see you at the meeting tonight.'

'Meeting?' Hodgkiss queried.

'Oh yes,' said Vera. 'I'd forgotten to tell them about it. I'm sure Edgar will want to go. Don't worry, Martha. We'll be there.'

'So what's it all about?' Hodgkiss asked after Mrs Meadows had gone.

Vera explained. 'The local council arranged it all. It's called a forum on tree care. Actually it will be the grand-father of all showdowns between the pro- and anti-loppers. Should be quite an event … if your nerves can stand it.'

'Sounds like something to look forward to,' said Hodgkiss. 'Nothing like a frank exchange of views.'

'I think you can be pretty sure it will be all of that … with the emphasis on the frank,' said Vera.

*　　*　　*

The meeting was held in the Masonic Hall, a tall building in the main street. The date 1845 was picked out in ornate brickwork high on the facade. The building was windowless apart from some narrow strips of dirty glass just beneath the eaves.

Hodgkiss smiled and dug Pat gently in the ribs, pointing up. 'They weren't about to risk curious folk spying on their secret ceremonies.'

Inside the main hall rows of seats had been arranged, but few were occupied. The audience was generally herded into two groups huddled on opposite sides of the central aisle. At the front of the hall a clergyman sat on a dais, an elderly woman seated beside him, a notebook open before her, a pencil in one hand.

Vera confided to Pat and Hodgkiss. 'Our parish priest and his housekeeper.'

'I wonder if either of them has had a letter,' Hodgkiss whispered.'

Vera shrugged. 'If they had we'd never hear about it.'

'Then you don't think the grapevine extends into the manse.'

'No way. But I've a feeling they'd come down heavily on the side of the anti-loppers.'

'Then you think it's mainly the loppers who've been getting mail.'

Vera nodded as the priest came to his feet.

He was a tall, thin man with a deep, resonating voice. 'Thank you for giving up your evening and coming out to take part in this important forum. You may be sure that I will be having something to say to those who did not find the time to be here this evening but who have nevertheless been perfectly willing to make their views known, often quite irresponsible views, I might add.'

There were murmurs of approval from the group, mainly women, who sat together on one side of the hall.

The priest held up a hand then continued. 'There is quite a number of people who have asked to speak so let's not waste time. First on my list is Mrs Meadows. There is no need to come up here, Martha. Just come to the front of the hall and say what you have your say.'

Martha Meadows made the most of her opportunity. She outlined the importance of trees as the lungs of the planet. She stressed the important place they played in combating global warming and in providing habitat for native species. She praised the local council for the comprehensive nature of its tree preservation code and complimented councillors on their determination to enforce it and for their public spirit in organizing the meeting.

When Mrs Meadows had returned to her seat, accompanied by a patter of applause, the priest announced: 'Mrs Graveney.'

A short, plump woman wriggled out of the row in front of where Hodgkiss was sitting and made her way to the front of the hall.

Mrs Graveney outlined her failed attempts to persuade council to allow her to remove a tree near her home which had on numerous occasions blocked her drains with its roots.

As she returned to her seat the priest remarked in jocular

manner; 'We all must do our best to keep Bert in work, mustn't we.'

Vera whispered. 'Bert is the local plumber,'

'Mrs Jennings is next on my list,' the priest announced, and continued; 'And Mrs Jennings, if you must repeat the story about your daughter's near-death experience please bear in mind that we are all well aware of what happened and keep it brief please.'

Mrs Jennings, a tall well-made woman in her forties, commented as she walked down the central aisle towards the front of the hall: 'People need reminding of how damned dangerous these bloody things can be.'

The priest adopted an expression of horror. 'Language please, Mrs Jennings. We may not be in God's house here but we should show respect to the feelings of others.'

Mrs Jennings replied with spirit. 'Yes, and we should show respect for the safety of others too. And I can see a couple of new faces among us tonight sitting with Vera Knight who wouldn't have heard how close my daughter came to being killed by that limb.'

She then recounted how she had written to the council on numerous occasions asking for permission to remove a large gum tree which overhung her home. When council refused she asked for permission to lop several branches but this too was refused. Then within a week of receiving the letter of rejection a limb had fallen from the tree striking her seventeen-year-old daughter breaking her collarbone. 'If she'd been standing a foot further to the right she'd be dead now,' Mrs Jennings said with a flourish. Then she recounted how she had written to council outlining her daughter's experience and asking again for permission to remove the tree but had not yet received a reply. That was more than a month ago. She finished with a few uncomplimentary remarks about those who sat on council then returned to her seat amid enthusiastic applause from her side of the hall.

The priest held up a hand to stay the applause then announced; 'Mrs Annabelle Fink is next.'

Vera groaned quietly. 'Oh no. This woman is quite potty.'

A tiny woman detached herself from the group on the other side of the hall and made her way quickly to the front.

Vera leaned across and whispered to Pat and Hodgkiss. 'Hold on to your seats. This will be a wild ride. This woman is definitely a sandwich short of a picnic.'

Hodgkiss listened with growing amazement to the woman's obviously well-rehearsed diatribe. A surprisingly deep voice rose from her diminutive frame.

'Some people speak lightly about tree lopping; the action of severing a limb from a tree. I don't call that lopping. I call it arboreal amputation.

'Some people speak casually about removing an entire tree. I have a special word for that … arborcide.'

She looked around aggressively as if daring someone in the audience to deny her definitions.

Hodgkiss heard Pat chuckle. She leaned towards him and whispered: 'Arborcide. Sounds like a crime committed at an 'arhouside mansion.'

Hodgkiss hissed. 'Careful, Pat. She's got her eye on you.'

Pat turned back quickly to find Miss Fink glowering at her.

'Apparently one of our visitors finds that amusing. No doubt she comes from Sydney where dozens of trees are murdered or mutilated every day.'

'That'll larn ya,' Hodgkiss hissed.

Miss Fink rolled on. 'Some people refuse to accept it when I tell them that I can actually hear trees crying out as their limbs are torn off by the hideous chainsaws, and later, after they limbs have been taken away for shredding, I hear their voices mourning for the lost limbs.

'And it is not the trees only I hear mourning. The birds too cry out for their lost homes.'

Then a voice from the back of the hall called. 'Next time you're talking to the trees tell them to be more careful where they drop their limbs.'

And another voice. 'And tell the birds there are plenty of trees left in my back yard … you old ratbag.'

The priest was on his feet. 'I will not have that kind of disrespectful interjection. It is an insult to a very sincere, intelligent and well-meaning woman.'

The first voice continued. 'And it's an insult to our intelligence to have to sit here and listen to this kind of insane twaddle. Arborcide! Arboreal amputation! I've never hears such rot! When someone hears voices we generally think they're loopy. But hearing trees' voices … trees crying out and moaning …loopy, that's the only word for it.'

The priest raised both arms in a theatrical gesture. 'I cannot allow these interruptions to continue. Miss Fink must be heard in silence.'

But Miss Fink had decided that she had said her piece and was returning to her place among her band of supporters who received her sympathetically.

The priest continued. 'I think after that little display of bad manners we might as well go home as I fail to see how anything productive can be achieved in the face of such intolerance. As chairman I will advise the town clerk, under whose auspices the forum was arranged, that I was most impressed by the force of the arguments presented by both sides, and I will mention that I was disappointed at the lengths that some present were prepared to go in order to prevent a fair presentation of arguments.'

The two groups began to leave the hall, careful not to mingle.

*   *   *

It was late the next morning when Vera, Pat and Hodgkiss assembled in Vera's kitchen overlooking the unmade road.

'I think that old-fashioned phrase "bats in the belfry" would cover the performance,' said Vera, taking a cautious sip of tea from her Dainty White Shelley teacup.

'One of the men sitting behind us preferred "loopy"' said Hodgkiss, 'but either one would do her justice.'

And so the postmortem continued rather repetitively until interrupted by the sound of a sharp whistle.

'Whatever was that?' Hodgkiss asked.

'That'll be Phillip, the postman. I'm rather surprised he wasn't at the meeting,' said Vera.

'You mean the postie still blows a whistle?' Pat asked, incredulous.

'Certainly does. Some of the old folk here have got quite a trek to their letterboxes and no sense in making the effort if there's nothing there.'

Hodgkiss pushed back his chair. 'There're one or two questions I'd like to ask Phillip the Postie,' he said, heading for the hall.

Through the kitchen window Vera and Pat saw Hodgkiss intercept the postman who was about to place a handful of mail in Vera's letterbox, which was in the form of a windmill.

They saw the two men shake hands and begin a conversation.

Phillip said. 'I've heard about you, Edgar. You'd be the detective fellah from Sydney who's staying with Vera.'

Hodgkiss tried to look modest. 'No, I'm not a detective. It's my son-in-law … he's the detective.'

'Maybe,' said Phillip. 'But you solve all his cases for him, right? Or so I've heard.'

'I do drop a hint now and then if I feel he's not on the right track.'

'And now you've come to Narrolong to solve our big mystery with the letters.' It was more a statement than a question.'

'That was the idea.'

'So how's it going? Have you solved it yet … who's writing the things?'

Hodgkiss shook his head. 'Early days yet. Vera seemed surprised that you weren't at the meeting last night.'

'Yeah, I was meaning to go but got held up. I suppose nutty old Miss Fink gave her usual Talking To The Trees speech, did she?'

'She certainly did. Quite amazing. But I suppose you've heard it all before.'

Phillip nodded. 'More than once.'

'So what held you up that made you miss the treat of hearing it all again?'

'Had a nasty little problem late in the afternoon,' said Phillip. 'Had to take a lady to hospital.'

'What happened? Did she have an accident?'

Phillip shook his head. 'It was no accident. It was all because of these damned letters.' He hesitated. 'I suppose it's all right to tell you, Edgar. seeing you're here to investigate the whole business.'

'Quite unofficially,' Hodgkiss stressed. 'I don't want you to tell me anything the post master general wouldn't approve of … if there was still such a person.'

'Oh no. It's nothing like that. Nothing you won't hear about anyway. I'm surprised it's not the talk of the town already. What happened was this: I was just finishing my round yesterday afternoon and I had two letters for Sergeant Flack. Well of course he was at the police station so I handed them to his wife at their house. I noticed that one of them looked like one of *those* letters. You can always tell them from the typing. Anyway, I handed it over and went off. But I'd gone no more than a few steps when I heard a kind of choking noise and turned around and there was Mrs Flack … she was holding on to the door post, then she just sort of slid down onto the doorstep. I thought she was having a fit or something. Anyway, I ran back, helped her up and took her inside. Then I called for the ambulance and they came and took her away to the hospital.'

'And the letter,' asked Hodgkiss. 'What happened to it?'

Phillip gave the matter some thought. 'I couldn't say for sure. Last I saw it was lying on the floor just inside the front door. When the ambulance arrived I just said goodbye and went on my round.'

Hodgkiss asked. 'Do you remember delivering one of *those* letters to Mr May … the fellow who died?'

Phillip shook his head. 'I've been asked that question a dozen times. They would have called me to give evidence at the inquest if I'd been able to give a straight answer one way or the other but I just couldn't, so the coroner decided there was no use calling me. Old May could have got one of course. He got a fair bit of mail and it could have been in a bundle I put in his box. Who can say? But the police didn't find one … or a suicide note, that is if he did commit suicide.'

'I believe it was put down to an accident,' said Hodgkiss.

'Yeah, but no one believes that. The coroner only said that because the parish priest wouldn't have buried him otherwise.'

Hodgkiss asked. 'Do you have any idea how many of these things you've delivered.'

Phillip shook his head. 'It's really hard to say. As I said there could have been one of them slipped in among others that I missed seeing.'

'But just roughly,' Hodgkiss pressed. 'Would it be five or more. Or, say, as many as ten perhaps.'

'It could be as many as ten … possibly more ,' Phillip conceded.

'And would you remember where you delivered them? You see, one of the problems with getting to grips with this business is that apparently no one has been reporting them to the police. Presumably they've just been tearing them up or throwing them away … apparently ignoring them. And of course if I can't examine a few of the things it makes it that much harder to get an idea of how to go about finding the culprit.'

Phillip nodded. 'Yes. I can see that. I tell you what. I'll have a think about it and see what I can remember. I'll give you a call.'

On that note the postman turned and went on his way with a wave and Hodgkiss returned inside.

*　　*　　*

'You mean Beth Flack is in the hospital?'

Vera was shocked at the news. 'I'm glad you found out, Edgar. I'll have to pay her a visit right away. She's one of my oldest friends. I was going to ring her after lunch to ask why she wasn't at the meeting.'

'Do you mind if we come too,' Hodgkiss asked.

Pat eyed him cautiously, shaking her head. 'I don't know if that's a very good idea.' She added, with an uneasy glance towards Vera. 'After all, we've never met the lady, and knowing you, Hodgkiss, you'd want to cross-examine her about the letter and she might not feel up to answering questions yet.'

'Oh I wouldn't worry about that, Pat,' said Vera. 'If Beth Flack doesn't feel up to coping with company she'll soon let us know. Wait a moment I'll get the car keys.'

'No need,' said Pat. 'My car's still outside.'

Five minutes later Pat was pulling on the handbrake in the forecourt of a large, two storey building at the top of the main street.

As she climbed out Pat observed: 'Well, if the whole of Narrolong went down with 'flu at the same time you'd have somewhere to treat them all.'

Vera nodded. 'Yes. There's an old story that this hospital was actually designed for a much larger town in Victoria somewhere, but the plans got mixed up and no one discovered the mistake until it was all too late.'

'I can believe it,' said Pat as the three entered the building.

A uniformed lady at a desk on the left of the cavernous entry hall informed them that Mrs Flack was in room 13 just down the corridor, but to see the sister at the nurses' station before entering the room seeing that visiting hours were over.

When they found the nurses' station deserted Vera tapped on the door of room 13 and the three filed in.

Beth Flack, a plump, cheerful woman in her mid-fifties, was sitting propped up against a mountain of pillows, reading.

'Excuse us barging in like this …' Vera began.

Beth Flack threw down her magazine. 'Vera. I was hoping you'd come to visit. I would have rung but they won't let me out of bed and the mobile won't work from here.' She turned to the others. 'And this is your cousin and the fellow must be the Sherlock Holmes type you told us about.'

The introductions were made and the visitors settled in seats that Hodgkiss brought in from an empty ward next door.

'I would have come sooner,' Vera explained, 'but I only just found out what had happened. Edgar heard about it from Phillip.'

'And thank goodness Phillip was there at the time,' said Beth. 'I really had quite a nasty turn.' Tears welled in her eyes. 'That awful letter.' She turned to Hodgkiss. 'I do hope you can do something about this business.'

'Do you know what became of the letter?' Hodgkiss asked. 'Phillip told me the last time he saw it it was lying on the floor just inside the front door.'

Beth shook her head. 'I've no idea what became of it. I know he handed it to me and I opened it straight away and started reading it. I knew from the strange typing on the envelope that it was one of those awful letters. I remember coming over all hot and it having difficulty breathing.' She put a hand to her chest. 'Next thing I knew I was sitting on the floor propped up against the door. I felt a bit of a fool really with Phillip fussing over me. Then the ambulance men came and they brought me here. There's nothing wrong with me of course. I suppose I just got a bit of a shock.'

'But the letter must have been pretty strong stuff to affect you like that,' said Vera. 'Do you remember what it said,' then she added hastily, 'that is if you don't mind telling us about it.'

'I only remember the little bit I read which was really very silly. It suggested that Ted and Constable Beasley were having an affair.'

'Constable Beasley is a fellow,' Vera explained quietly to Hodgkiss.

'The whole idea's absurd,' said Beth. 'Why, Constable Beasley is the captain of the local Rugby team.'

'Absurd!' Hodgkiss echoed. 'So you've no idea where the letter might be.'

Beth shrugged. 'No. I suppose you could ask the ambulance fellows if they saw it. Failing that, Ted might have it. After all, if it was lying on the floor in the hall Ted must have seen it when he came home last night. Oh, and here he is now. We were just talkin about you, Ted.'

Hodgkiss turned to see a large man standing in the doorway. He was dressed in police uniform with three stripes on both sleeves.'

Beth continued: 'Come on in Ted and meet Vera's friends.'

Vera made the introductions then Ted delivered a firm kiss to his wife's cheek and perched on the edge of the bed.

'You'll have to hop off if nurse comes,' Beth warned. 'Meanwhile, I'm sure Mr Hodgkiss here … Edgar … has a few questions for you. In fact we were wondering whether or not you saw that awful letter lying in the hall where I dropped it.'

Ted nodded. 'Yes. It was the first thing I saw when I came through the door. Bloody nasty-minded creeps. I didn't tell the Constable Jack what was in it. It'd've really upset him.'

'Apart from that one do you have any other letters?' Hodgkiss asked.

'Yes, I have now, Edgar. After I saw that letter I made a point of going around a few of the locals and started collecting them.'

'So you knew who had received them.'

'Yeah. There are no secrets in Narrolong. I thought so long as they didn't want to make a fuss about it I'd ignore it. But when I saw Beth's letter I thought I just couldn't let sleeping dogs lie any longer so I went around and gathered them up and Constable Jack has sent them off to forensics for fingerprinting. I kept copies at the station because I thought you might like to have a look at them, Edgar. Beth said that Vera had mentioned that your son-in-law was a detective and that you'd been pretty handy at helping him work things out.'

'I'd certainly appreciate it if I could have a look at some examples to see what, if anything, I can make of them.'

At that moment the door swung inwards and a woman in a blue uniform came in, pulling behind her a large steel trolley bearing two steaming urns and trays of cups and saucers.

'Tea or coffee?' she asked.

*　　*　　*

Pat parked the Mercedes beside the highway patrol car in the parking area behind the police station which was next door to the hospital.

Pat, Hodgkiss and Vera followed Sergeant Flack into the police station through a rear entry.

The sergeant led the way to a large office at the front of the building with a commanding view of the main street.

'Take a seat,' he said, 'and I'll bring in the photocopies and see what you can make of them.'

He disappeared into the hall and returned moments later with a bundle of plastic folders. He handed them to Hodgkiss who, with the others, had settled around a long old-fashioned wooden table.

Sergeant Flack explained. 'As I said, the originals have been sent off for forensic examination. I had a go at them with some of the gear I have here and there was certainly no shortage of prints on them. The thing is, will they enable us to get a lead on who actually made the things. Frankly I doubt it.'

'Why's that, Sergeant?' Vera asked.

Sergeant Flack shrugged. 'When something's covered with prints and partial prints all spotted one on top of the other it can be near impossible to say who handled the things last.'

He brightened. 'But I can tell you a few things that might prove of interest. The first is that the envelopes were all typed on the same typewriter.'

Hodgkiss asked. 'Have you been able to ascertain what kind of typewriter was used?'

'*I* haven't, but the boys at forensic no doubt will be able to pinpoint that. All I can tell you is that it was an old one that had had a lot of use. Two of the letters were out of alignment. Others were worn. For instance, the tail on the p on one of the machines had almost disappeared and the centre of the top of the lower case e was filled in. That was on the typewriter used for the envelopes.'

'And the letters?'

'With them I'd say there were three different typewriters used. Have a look for yourselves. You'll see that there are lots of little imperfections in the type that suggest three different machines were used. That's just my opinion but of course I'm no expert.'

'I'd be happy to take your word on it, sergeant, for the time being,' said Hodgkiss. He picked up one of the plastic folders and pointed to the document inside.

'This one appears to have been done with a very faint ribbon which suggests it was either very old and dry or much used.'

'Yes, I noticed that, Edgar. You'll find there's another letter done on the same machine where the print is very black, which suggests that whoever did it had changed the ribbon which of course means that she, or possibly he, had a spare ribbon or bought a new one. Now, I've asked at the local paper shop which is the only place in town likely to stock something like that, and the fellow there said he hadn't stocked typewriter ribbons for years.'

'Hardly surprising,' said Vera. 'These days he probably sells things like toner cartridges for computer printers.'

'And another thing,' said Sergeant Flack. 'In two cases whoever did it put the wrong letter in one of the envelopes.'

Hodgkiss asked. 'Really? How do you know that?'

Sergeant Flack searched among the plastic envelopes which Hodgkiss had spread around on top of the table.

'Here. This one. You'll notice I've kept the envelope together with the letter that it contained. In this one the envelope is address to Mrs J Emerson but the letter inside it starts: 'Dear Mr Marks.' Actually this one is a good example of how the writer went about his or her job.'

'Job?' Pat queried 'What do you mean job"?'

'I mean the way he got his message across. They are all pretty uniform; first comes the nasty threatening part then the message, in this case as with all the letters, the message is usually much the same: 'you are one of those people in favour of lopping trees and if you don't change your evil ways I will expose you as a" … whatever the letter threatens to tell. You'll see what I mean in the case of the letter to Mr Marks who is the manager of our local branch of the State Bank.

'It starts: "Dear Mr Marks, I suppose you think you were clever about the way you cheated poor old Mr Ems out of his farm. Everyone knows you only called in his debt and sold him up so that your brother-in-law could come in and buy the farm up at a bargain basement price. The sort of despicable behaviour one would expect from one who sees nothing wrong with cutting down wonderful trees in the prime of their life. Don't think you'll be able to keep this hidden for ever. Mend your ways or the truth will come out."'

Sergeant Flack put down the plastic envelope and picked up another.

'Here's another prime example. It was sent to Mr Friend who runs the greengrocers. "Dear Mr Friend. Not a very appropriate name for someone who behaves like you. Everyone knows that you made poor Mrs Everingham broke when you stopped taking her eggs and other produce because she made her daughter stop seeing you to save her from your lustful behaviour. No one is surprised that a wicked person such as you would also accept, even encourage the thoughtless destruction of trees in our village. You may think you have been clever in keeping your affair with that girl quiet but I will take steps to see that everyone, particularly your wife and daughter, are informed of your behaviour if you do not change your attitudes."'

Hodgkiss nodded. 'I see. The pattern is the same: the sinful conduct is outlined then comes the threat of exposure unless attitudes towards trees changes. Bizarre. Quite bizarre.'

'The others are similar,' said Sergeant Flack. 'And in most, no, all of the letters I have read the "sinful conduct" as you call it, is generally pretty well spot on. There was a lot of talk about six months ago about how Marks at the bank foreclosed on one of his loans and a relation, it may have been a brother-in-law as the letter claims, came in and bought up the property cheap. It didn't even go on the open market, or so I'm told. I didn't know about it at the time. It was done very quietly. The farm was a few miles out of town and it all happened before anyone knew anything about it.'

'Nasty,' said Vera. 'If there was another bank in town I'd switch.'

'What about the other letter?' Hodgkiss asked. 'Mrs Everingham's daughter and the lustful greengrocer? Any truth in that?'

Sergeant Flack nodded vigourously. 'Oh yes. But everyone knew about that.'

'So the threat to tell his wife and daughter was hollow?'

'I don't know about that. The Everingham's split up last year and he moved away so he may not have known about it and it certainly would have done her no good if he'd found out because I understand they're going to court and if there was some suggestion of the mother allowing the daughter to play up with a married man ... well, it might put her in a weak bargaining position when it came to court hearings. You never know with these things.'

'So these were not idle threats in these two cases?' Hodgkiss asked.

'They were not. And I'd say the threats in the other letters here aren't idle threats either. Whoever wrote them knew what was happening around town.'

'And what about Arthur May. The fellow whose funeral we saw on our way into town yesterday? Do we know what he was threatened with?'

Sergeant Flack shook his head. 'Nothing definite, I'm afraid Edgar, unless it was the other one of the letters that somehow got into the wrong envelope that was intended for him. Wait a moment, I'll find it.'

Sergeant Flack began sorting through the plastic envelopes on the table.

'Ah, here it is. You see the envelope was addressed to Mrs Averill Hahn. When I collected it from her she told me the letter had nothing to do with her and I believe her because she doesn't have a dog, as stated in the letter. And the letter has no greeting at the top of the letter to say it was for her or for anyone in particular. It just starts: "Cheats never prosper.'

'So we are left to conclude that the particular sin in this case was infidelity?'

'Not much doubt about that, Edgar. This is how it goes on: "I suppose you think that no one has noticed you taking your little dog for rather long walks on the same nights each week. It is very thoughtless of you to leave the poor little fellow tied up for so long outside the school house while you engage in sinful conduct. Your wife would be horrified if knew." Then there's the usual punch line about how he doesn't care about people lopping trees and he that should mend his ways if he doesn't want the truth to come out.'

Hodgkiss asked. 'I assume Mr May had a dog.'

'Yes, he did. A Jack Russell. He's still in the pound, poor little fellow.'

'And was Mr May in the habit of taking long walks on particular nights?'

Sergeant Flack shrugged. 'Not so far as I know. He was a rather nice old guy who kept to himself. His wife had been in a home for a while. Dementia. Quite gaga, or so I'm told.'

'Then the threat to tell his wife would have been pretty hollow.'

Yes, I suppose it would. Still you never know. Old Mr May might have taken it seriously.'

'I understand there's some doubt about whether or not the fellow took his own life?'

The sergeant shook his head. 'Who knows? There was no suicide note, or should I say we didn't find one, and there's no suggestion he'd been depressed lately. But there was a lot of talk about it being suicide, heaven alone knows how the talk started, and the parish priest had to be convinced that suicide was out of the question or he would never have agreed to bury him.'

'Anything else of particular interest?' Hodgkiss asked.

The sergeant shook his head. 'I don't imagine we'll have anything new to go on until we get the results from the forensic people. Until then I'd say we've done about as much as we can. That is unless you have some ideas, Edgar?'

Hodgkiss frowned. 'I agree there's not much we can do for the moment, but I'd be very curious to know where on earth all these typewriters came from. Somewhere in Narrolong … or very close nearby … there are at least three old-fashioned typewriters sitting around. It is most unlikely that they were always in the same place at the same time as they appear to be at present if all these letters and envelopes were prepared by the same person. I mean to say … who owns three old-fashioned typewriters?'

'I can tell you that," said Vera. 'The Narrolong Secretarial School. Or it used to. I know that because I learned typing there more years ago than I care to remember.'

'I remember the Secretarial School,' said Sergeant Flack. 'It was at the back of the council chambers. But it closed down years ago.'

'Yes, but what happened to the typewriters? Hodgkiss asked. 'Were they sent to the tip. Somehow I think that unlikely. Typewriters were rather expensive items in their day. Does anyone remember who ran this Secretarial School?'

'Yes, I remember,' said Vera. 'Her name was Miss White and so far as I know she still lives in town.'

'Excellent,' said Hodgkiss. 'Then let us pay Miss White a visit.'

'It's not at all far from here,' said Vera. 'Easy walking distance.'

*   *   *

As Vera led the way down the main street towards the railway station Hodgkiss remarked: 'You know that letter to Mr May about tying his dog up outside the school house at night …'

'Yes, what about it?' Vera asked.

'Well, it could have had nothing to do with him committing suicide, could it? I mean … he would never have received it. It was addressed to someone called J Emerson.'

'Yes, I remember that, Edgar, but it doesn't mean a thing. If that letter went to Jenny Emerson then it would only have been an hour or two at the most before the whole of Narrolong knew everything that was in it. Jenny is known as the Town Crier. If you want some news spread around town you only have to tell Jenny.'

Hodgkiss shook his head, disappointed. 'Another theory out the window.'

'At least someone's developing theories,' said Pat. 'I haven't got a clue who's writing the things.'

'Oh I don't think there's much doubt about that,' said Hodgkiss. 'But of course we have to find the evidence. That's a different matter altogether.'

Vera stopped short and turned to Hodgkiss. 'You mean to say you think you know who's writing these letters?'

'Of course,' said Hodgkiss. 'There can be no doubt about it.'

'Then who is it. For heaven's sake, tell us.'

Pat shook her head. 'No use trying to make him say a word 'til he's good and ready. He has a favourite saying for these situation; "I will not put my cards on the table …"'

'" … until I have filled my hand,"' Hodgkiss finished.

'It's a phrase that would be familiar to anyone who plays rummy,' Pat explained.

'So you enjoy a game of rummy, do you Edgar? Vera asked.

'Yes, I do,' said Hodgkiss, 'when I can find someone why actually knows the rules of the game.'

Pat rolled her eyes. 'Whenever we have a game the name of Hoyle is mentioned quite a lot … particularly when Hodgkiss is losing.'

Vera chuckled. 'I get the picture.' She turned to Hodgkiss. 'So how long before you "fill your hand", Edgar?' she asked.

'Oh quite soon, I think,' said Hodgkiss, watching a magpie pecking at a piece of something on the nature strip outside the house where they had stopped.' He added. 'Narrolong isn't a very big place. There can't be too many suspects.'

'I wouldn't be too sure of that,' said Vera. 'Once you've scratched the surface I think you'll find more than one person who needs a second glance. Now, this is where Miss White lives,' she said. 'And that's her, on the verandah.'

The house was a classic Federation bungalow; high off the ground on sandstone block foundations with wide well worn steps leading up to a tessellated veranda that ran halfway around the house.

Miss White, a tiny woman with a huge cloud of silver hair, was sitting in a cane chair on the verandah. She rose as the three climbed the steps.

'These must be your visitors from the Big Smoke, Vera. And this one would be the famous detective,' she said, extending a hand towards Hodgkiss.

'I'm afraid I'm nothing of the kind,' said Hodgkiss taking the hand. 'To paraphrase the American wit who was surprised by his own obituary; 'Reports of my detective talents have been greatly exaggerated."'

'Well, that remains to be seen,' said Miss White, pushing the front door open and leading the way into a long, dim hallway. 'Reports around town say that you've been very busy since you arrived.'

Vera said: 'He has a theory about who's writing the things but, to use his excuse, he won't put his cards on the table until he's "filled his hand".'

'Quite right and proper too,' said Miss White. 'It would never do to blame the innocent.'

Hodgkiss nodded agreement. 'Precisely, Miss White. People sometimes overlook that aspect of things. That kind of damage, once done, is not easily undone.'

They declined an offer of tea or coffee and soon were settled in the front room, crowded with dark Victorian furniture and the walls crammed with small bad watercolour paintings.

'Now,' said Miss White, 'is there some way I can help to advance your investigation, Mr Hodgkiss. I assume that is why you are here.'

'You assume correctly, Miss White,' said Hodgkiss 'As you probably are aware these offensive letters are all written on old fashioned typewriters.'

'Ah. I notice you say "typewriters" plural. So more than one typewriter is involved, is it?' asked Miss White. 'Interesting. So obviously you think of me … the previous owner of a large number of typewriters. Logical enough, I suppose.'

'Well, that saves explaining,' said Hodgkiss.

'Yes, but if your logic has led you to the conclusion that I have been writing the letters then further explanation is necessary,' Miss White said with a smile.

Hodgkiss held up a hand. 'I assure you, Miss White, that you are not under suspicion for anything. We came here in the hope that you may know the present whereabouts of the typewriters formerly used in your secretary school.'

Miss White nodded. 'Well, there is no big mystery about

that, Mr Hodgkiss. When what was ludicrously termed "The March of Progress" rendered the duties of the trained secretary obsolete my business declined sharply.' She turned to Vera. 'You, I think, were in one of my last classes.'

Vera nodded. 'And I can still type and write shorthand fast enough to take down the news off the radio.'

Miss White smiled. 'Yes. I remember you were one of my more talented students. I think you were in the same class as Miss Fink, but she was never up to your standard. However, all good things must end and I put all my goods to auction: the typewriters of course, the text books I provided for typing and shorthand ... although of course there was not much of a market for them ... and the desks and chairs as well. I won't say they realised a great deal of money because they didn't. However I already had this home and a nest egg big enough to keep me comfortably.'

'And the typewriters?' Hodgkiss asked. 'Do you remember who bought them?'

'I certainly do. Everything was bought by a local charitable group.'

'And do you know what they did with them?'

'I know that they planned to teach shorthand and typing to local children but of course nothing came of it. No one was really interested and it just folded up.'

'Then what became of all the equipment ... the typewriters, books, desks etcetera?'

'They were all donated to the school ... I suppose they're all still there somewhere unless they've disposed of them.'

'All that equipment would take up a lot of space, wouldn't it. It must be rather inconvenient for the school to have to store it all if they'd got no use for it.'

Miss White nodded. 'I expect you're right. Of course

the typewriters were all properly boxed up individually by the removalists when they took them away from my establishment to auction, so they wouldn't take up too much space because they could be properly stacked. But desks and chairs are another matter.'

'And exactly how many typewriters went to auction?' Hodgkiss asked.

Miss White replied with pride. 'I had thirty-five typewriters. The best quality and latest models. I was very proud of them and it was something of a wrench seeing them going off to be sold. I remember checking the boxes off as the men took them away … thirty-five.'

'And some charitable organisation bought them?'

'Yes, I can't remember the exact name, but it was run by Miss Fink. Have you met her yet?'

Hodgkiss looked up in surprise. 'The anti-tree lopping woman?'

'That's the one. She could probably tell you more about what became of the typewriters than I.'

Hodgkiss nodded. 'I dare say.' He turned to the others. 'I think we should have a word with that lady … without delay.'

'Do you know where she lives?' Miss White asked.

Vera replied. 'She used to live opposite the school. I haven't heard that she moved so I suppose she still there?'

Miss White nodded. 'She hasn't moved. She'd never leave her trees.'

Vera got to her feet. 'Come on you two. It's only a short walk.'

*   *   *

Vera led the way up the main street, almost to the top where the school stood on the corner of an unmade road running a short distance to the left.

As they turned the corner Vera indicated a small wooden cottage, almost covered by vines which stood on the corner opposite the school.

'Alf Graham lives in there. A dear old fellow but as deaf as a post which is just as well in some ways because the school boys have composed some rather naughty songs which they sing about him as they walk past.'

'And who lives next door there?' Hodgkiss asked, indicating a rather more elaborate wooden bungalow, the only other house in the street, which stood next door to the corner house and opposite the side of the school.'

'That's Miss Fink's. The woman we saw perform at the meeting last night. She lives there.'

'Does she indeed,' said Hodgkiss, pausing to subject the building to a close scrutiny. 'Rather fond of pot plants, isn't she,' he remarked, indicating a row of five pots on the front verandah, each standing on what looked like small wooden stools.

He pushed back the chain wire gate. 'I'd like a word with Ms Fink. There're one or two questions I'd like to ask her'

He walked smartly up to the front door and plied the brass knocker vigourously while the two women waited awkwardly on the footpath.

'Don't come on too strong, Hodgkiss,' Pat cautioned in a loud hiss. 'After all we're visitors in town … and Vera's guests.'

Hodgkiss saw a tiny movement in a lace curtain in the front window, but his summons went unanswered.

He returned down the front path announcing in a voice designed to be heard at a distance: 'She's in there all right. Just doesn't want to come to the door.'

Pat nodded agreement. 'Yes. I saw the curtain too. Maybe later.'

Vera said. 'While we're here we might as well have a word to Edwina Foster, the school teacher.'

'And alleged lover of the late Mr May,' Hodgkiss muttered. He continued. 'And correct me if I'm wrong, Vera, but didn't you mention that Mrs Meadows also teaches at the school?'

Vera nodded. 'That's so Edgar, although I couldn't tell you what subjects she teaches.'

'No doubt her syllabus would include material relating to the preservation of trees and possibly all vegetable matter.'

As they approached a small cottage behind the school building Vera said, 'Since it's school holidays Edwina is probably in the cottage.

Hodgkiss said. 'The same cottage where Mr May is supposed to have tied up his dog on the frequent nocturnal visits he is alleged to have made.' He turned and glanced back over the road. 'And of course Miss Fink is ideally placed to keep the school cottage under surveillance … day and night.'

Hodgkiss turned back in time to see Edwina Foster open the front door of the cottage and step out. 'Good morning Vera. And these are your visitors from Sydney. Please come in.'

Vera made the introductions and the three followed Edwina into the cottage and down a central hall to a kitchen at the rear which commanded a view over the school playground.

'I had the kettle on so please join me,' she said, pouring boiling water into a large floral teapot. 'And if Mr Hodgkiss has any questions for me I'd be delighted to assist him with his inquiries, as the saying goes.' She turned, smiling. 'That is, of course if the stories about your talents as a detective are true.'

'The stories are true enough,' said Vera. 'He may have

questions for you, but I think they can wait for the time being. At least until we've had our tea.'

Hodgkiss blew across the top of his teacup, sipped cautiously and said: 'I do have one or two questions for you Edwina, but I think I would learn more if I could make a quick inspection of your storeroom or where ever it is you keep all of those typewriters that were donated to the school.'

Edwina looked up, surprised. 'The typewriters. You want to see them. Well, there's no problem about that. They're still in the storeroom where the removalists put them years ago and I doubt if anyone's touched them since. As a gift they were a white elephant in the true meaning of the words. More of a problem than an asset. They've just been sitting there for years taking up space. I suppose it's lucky were not short of space or I'd have had to get rid of the things.'

'Do you remember how many typewriters were donated?' Hodgkiss asked.

Edwina shook her head. 'It all happened well before my time, but I could check the records. It'd only take a moment.'

'I take it that no one ever took them out and tried to teach the children how to type?'

'Not that I've ever heard about. Perhaps Mrs Meadows would be able to tell you. She used to teach here before I arrived.'

'And does she still teach?'

'No. Not really. On the days she comes she supervises the children in the playground or reads to them when I'm holding a class for the more advanced ones.'

'So she isn't officially on staff?' Hodgkiss asked.

'Depends what you mean by "officially on staff". She is certainly on the payroll although she doesn't get paid a great deal. With her I think it is more a matter of prestige ... being able to say she's a teacher.'

'I suppose what I want to know is whether or not Mrs Meadows would have the keys to the store room ... where the old typewriters are kept.'

Edwina hesitated. 'I don't know what she or anybody would want with the old typewriters ...' Then. 'Oh, I see what you're getting at.' She paused. 'If Mrs Meadows wanted to access the typewriters for any reason she wouldn't need a key. The key to the storeroom was lost years ago and nobody ever bothered the lock changed or a new key made because there is nothing of value in the storeroom ... including the typewriters. Nobody wants them ... or rather I suppose somebody wants them until now if you think they've been used for these poison pen letters that have been going about.'.

'That, of course, is exactly what I think. Now, would you mind if I had a look around the storeroom.'

'No problem, Mr Hodgkiss.' She pushed back her chair and rose. 'Come with me. It's attached to the rear of the school.'

Hodgkiss followed Edwina out into the playground then across to the rear of the school. She pulled open a door at the back of the building and the two went inside into what appeared to be an administration office.

'This is my office, Edgar. The store room is through this door,' Edwina said indicating a metal door to one side of the room.

She pulled the handle down and pulled the door back. She stepped into the room, reached around and turned on the lights.

Hodgkiss stepped forward and looked in.

Much of the space was taken up by square packing cases.

'Have you counted them any chance?' Hodgkiss asked.

Edwina shook her head. "Fraid not. How many should there be, do you know?'

'According to Miss White, who used to run the secretarial school where they were used, there were thirty five when she sent them to auction. So let's count them. It looks to me as if they are stacked in lots of five so there should be seven stacks. Right?'

'Sounds right to me,' said Edwina. She stepped into the room and began counting. 'Seven stacks there are, and five in each stack. Thirty five if my maths are correct.'

'Well that was simple enough,' said Hodgkiss. 'Now for the not-so-simple part.'

'You mean checking to see that all the typewriters are still in their boxes?' Edwina asked.'

'Right on the money,' said Hodgkiss. 'It should be simple enough to tell if any of the boxes have been opened, that is assuming that all of the boxes contained their typewriters when they were delivered here from the auction or wherever they were when Ms Fink decided to give the school this rather inopportune gift.'

'Don't you think the delivery men might have noticed if some of the boxes had been opened and the typewriters removed.'

'I dare say,' said Hodgkiss. 'However, they may have noticed but not thought anything of it. They simply had to deliver them ... empty or full. It wasn't any business of theirs. So I fear we are going to have to check for ourselves. I'll start at this end. I think it would speed things up if you could find a couple of sharp implements to cut the tape.'

Edwina protested. 'But why not just lift them up. If one of them doesn't have the typewriter in it you'll soon notice.'

Hodgkiss nodded. 'Yes, but whoever did it may have replaced it with something of a similar weight.'

Edwina began. 'Yes, but that would mean that ...'

Hodgkiss nodded. 'Exactly. I think we need to look inside.'

As soon as Edwina had disappeared into the outer office Hodgkiss hurried across the room to a bank of shelves built against a side wall. On the shelves were stacks of old text books.

Two of the stacks were of old text books devoted to instruction in touch typing. Both books on the top of the stacks were covered by a fine film of dust.

The other two stacks, much smaller volumes, gave instruction in Pitman's shorthand and the top volume in one of these stacks was free of dust.

Thoughtfully, Hodgkiss ran a finger over the book.

Then a sound made him turn to see Edwina standing in the door to the office, watching him anxiously. In her hands were two sharp Stanley knives.

'Thinking of learning shorthand, Edgar?' she inquired casually. Then she held up the knives. 'These should do the trick,' she said.

The two set to work cutting the tape across the top of the boxes, opening the boxes and checking the contents.

When Hodgkiss had opened his first box he lifted out a small wooden item built along the lines of a platform and held it out to Edwina.

'This was in the box with the typewriter. Have you any idea why it would have been there?'

Edwina nodded. 'Yes. Someone told me that those wooden bridge things were used in the typing classes. As the girls became more and more proficient they were place over the keyboard so they couldn't see when they typed.'

Hodgkiss nodded. 'There are five on Miss Fink's front verandah. She has pot plants sitting on them.'

Edwina looked up, surprised, then she shrugged. 'I

suppose she might have hung on to them when she sent the typewriters off to auction.'

'Yes, she might. Or she might have come over here and pinched them along with the typewriters. Not a very difficult task seeing that there's not a locked door in the whole place.'

'I can't see Miss Fink coming over here in the middle of the night, cutting open boxes and carrying five typewriters and those wooden things home with her, although I suppose she might not have done it all on her own or necessarily on the one night. I was away on two weeks holidays last year and she could have done it then and taken her time I suppose. The place would have been deserted.'

'She could have had help from one of her arboreal allies,' said Hodgkiss. 'Anyway, for the present let's get on and see if we can find any boxes that have been opened and the contents removed.'

It was less than two minutes before Edwina called. 'Bingo, Edgar. This one's empty. And so is this one and these ones,' she said as she picked the boxes up one by one then set them down again. 'Five of them. All quite empty. And you can see where the tape has been cut and put back in place rather untidily.'

Hodgkiss nodded. 'Then I think we had better have a serious talk with Miss Fink. She has a lot of explaining to do, wouldn't you say?'

Edwina held up a hand. 'Before we go anywhere or do anything there's something you should know.'

'About the letters?'

'Yes. Oh, don't worry, I had nothing to do with writing them.'

'But you heard about the one suggesting impropriety between Mr May and yourself ... his dog being tied up outside at night.'

'Yes, of course. News of that was all around town. Mothers were keeping their children home from school on account of it. They said that I wasn't a fit person to be teaching their children. This is a very narrow-minded little place in many ways.'

'You don't need to convince me of that. I've seen it at work already. It is not a place brimming over with Christian charity and the spirit of forgiveness. So what did you do, Edwina?'

'When I heard about the letter that apparently went to the wrong person ... that is, not to Arthur ... I went to see him.'

'And what did he advise?'

'He didn't advise anything. He was dead.' She dropped her eyes. 'The poor man had killed himself.'

'Killed himself!? How can you be sure?'

'He left a note. I kept it.'

'Because you knew the priest would never give him a proper burial if the inquest found suicide.'

She nodded. 'Now I suppose the police will have to know.'

Hodgkiss shook his head thoughtfully. 'I don't see why. The inquest was held and a finding given. That chapter is closed. The second chapter ... the wicked letters ... putting an end to them ... that's what's important now. That's the chapter we must write an ending to.'

'Won't you have to tell Vera and your friend Pat about the note?'

Hodgkiss shrugged. 'Eventually ... possibly. But I can't think of any reason why they would want to tell anyone or make trouble for you. You've been through enough already. I strongly suggest that you destroy it without delay.'

Edwina nodded. 'So what do we do now, Edgar?'

'I'll have to talk to Sergeant Flack. I think it's about time to hand the whole thing over to them. I'd rather they dealt with Miss Fink although it may not be easy to get a search warrant to look for the typewriters in her house just on the basis of what we've discovered here.'

The two returned to the school cottage where Vera and Pat had tidied away the things from afternoon tea.

Hodgkiss asked. 'Vera, can you ring the police station. I need to talk to the sergeant rather urgently.'

Vera shot a curious look at Hodgkiss but made the call without question. After a short conversation with the constable she announced. 'Sergeant Flack is at the hospital with his wife. Apparently it's visiting hours.'

'Excellent,' said Hodgkiss. 'Then let's visit. Are you coming Edwina?'

Edwina shook her head. 'I'd rather stay here if you wouldn't mind. I've got a few things to think over … and one thing I've got to do.'

*   *   *

'Well, we're all certainly getting our exercise with all the walking we've been doing,' Hodgkiss observed as he, Pat and Vera walked back along the main road towards the hospital where they made their way to Beth Flack's room.

'Come in,' Beth called when Vera knocked. 'Goodness, I'm very popular this evening,' she added when the three filed in. She indicated where Mrs Meadows stood at the end of the bed. 'Martha called in earlier to see how I was coming along and of course Ted came in to pick up my washing.'

Sergeant Flack was standing behind the door with a large bulging plastic bag on the floor beside him.

'I'm just the housemaid these days,' he said ruefully to Hodgkiss who clucked sympathetically.

Martha Meadows picked up her hand bag from the bed. 'Well, I'll be getting on my way, Beth. You've got plenty of company now. It's good to see you looking your old self.'

Hodgkiss quickly positioned himself between Mrs Meadows and the door. 'If you wouldn't mind staying a moment longer, Mrs Meadows.'

'Really, Mr Hodgkiss,' Martha protested. 'I have an appointment. I'd better be on my way.'

'Very well, Mrs Meadows, but before you go I'm sure you can find a moment to explain to Sergeant Flack why you sent him that most unpleasant letter suggesting an improper relationship between him and his constable?'

There was a moment's silence. Everyone froze. First they turned to look at Hodgkiss, then at Sergeant Flack and finally at Mrs Meadows.

'Well,' said Hodgkiss, eyeing Mrs Meadows sternly. 'We're all waiting to hear your explanation.'

'But that's nonsense,' she gushed. 'I didn't write a letter to the sergeant. I didn't write letters to anyone. I don't know why you'd think such a thing.'

'Don't you, Mrs Meadows. Then perhaps you would like me to tell you.'

But Mrs Meadows said nothing, standing stock still, gripping her handbag defensively before her.

'No? Well I'll tell you anyway,' said Hodgkiss. 'Besides, I'm sure all these people would like to know ... particularly Sergeant Flack. You'd like to know, wouldn't you, sergeant.'

Sergeant Flack recovered himself sufficiently to nod agreement.

Hodgkiss began. 'I remember the morning after Pat and arrived in Narrolong we were sitting having morning tea with Cousin Vera and we saw you coming down the pathway. Of course you came in and you were full of all sorts of news. And during the course of the conversation you told us that Sergeant Flack had received one of those disgusting letters.'

'That's true,' said Vera. 'I distinctly remember that because you said the same thing the day before when we saw you down in the town … you told us that Sergeant Flack had received one of the letters.'

Hodgkiss continued. 'And the truth is that Sergeant did not receive the letter until the day after your visit to Vera's house; that is the morning after Pat and I arrived in Narrolong.

'So the question is this; how did you know about Sergeant Flack's letter at least two days before he received it?'

Mrs Meadows shook her head vigourously from side to side. 'No. No. You must have misunderstood. I didn't say that he'd received a letter at all. I couldn't have said that. I couldn't have. I might have said he could receive a letter … or that he might receive a letter.'

Hodgkiss shook his head. 'But you didn't, Mrs Meadows,' he said quietly. 'Vera and I and Pat … we all heard you. He *had* received a letter. That's what you said. You really need to explain how you knew about it before it happened. We are not accusing you of writing the letter, Mrs Meadows, but it is perfectly plain that you knew a letter had been written or was to be written and sent to Sergeant Flack.'

Mrs Meadows drew herself up. 'I can't say. I really can't. It's quite ridiculous you accusing me of such a thing.'

Hodgkiss began speaking with a quiet menace. 'The time for games is over, Mrs Meadows. By your unguarded remarks, to which there are reliable witnesses, you have placed yourself in an invidious position. If you do not have an explanation for your actions I think Sergeant Flack will have no choice but to take you to the police station and ask you to make a formal statement on the matter. Pat, Vera and I will also make sworn statements about what you said and when you said it. Then it will then be up to the appropriate authorities to decide whether or not a prosecution should be launched.'

'But this is ridiculous,' Mrs Meadows blustered. 'I never wrote any of those letters. I swear. I'll swear a statement to that.'

Hodgkiss shook his head gently. 'You misunderstand me, Mrs Meadows. No one is accusing you of writing those letters. No one said that. I certainly did not say it. BUT YOU KNEW. You knew that someone was going to write a malicious letter to the sergeant. You cannot deny it? Who was it, Mrs Meadows. Who was it?'

Mrs Meadows stood in the room breathing heavily, struck dumb.

Hodgkiss continued. 'Very well, Mrs Meadows. If you won't give us the name of the letter writer let *me* give *you* the name.'

Mrs Meadows looked up at Hodgkiss. Her lips moved but no sound came out.

'It was Miss Fink, wasn't it?' Hodgkiss said. 'You knew she meant to write the letter to Sergeant Flack, but something happened ... there was a delay and she didn't tell you. Isn't that true?'

Mrs Meadows nodded slowly.

Hodgkiss turned to Vera. 'Then I think we have one more visit to make ... one more walk to take ... then we can call it a day.'

*   *   *

Soon the three were walking once more down the main street towards the railway station.

It was dark now and the street was empty. At the school they turned into the side street and past the corner cottage.

The light was on in Miss Fink's front room.

'She can't pretend not to be home this time,' Hodgkiss said.

As they approached Miss Finks bungalow Hodgkiss held up a hand and the group stopped.

'Listen, what's that sound?' Hodgkiss asked in a whisper.

'It sounds like someone crying,' Vera hissed.

Hodgkiss waved a hand forward and the three proceeded on tiptoe.

When they reached the front gate to Miss Fink's house Hodgkiss signaled for the others to stay where they were while opened the gate quietly.

A woman's voice came through the dark. 'Is that you, Constable?'

'No. Is that you Edwina?' Hodgkiss asked.

'Yes. Mr Hodgkiss is it? Oh I'm so glad you've come. I rang the police station and left a message for the constable to come as quickly as possible.'

Hodgkiss hurried down the path towards the verandah. 'Why, what's the problem? What's happened?'

Then he saw Edwina sitting on a bench seat on the verandah. 'Whatever happened to your face?'

Edwina raised a hand to a face streaked with blood. 'I ... there's been an accident. It's Miss Fink. I think she's dead.'

Hodgkiss crossed the verandah and entered the hall. The door to a living room to the right was open. Miss Fink was stretched on the polished boards of the living room floor.

Blood had pooled from a nasty gash in the side of her head.

Hodgkiss hurried into the room and stooped beside the figure. He placed a hand on the thin, pale neck and felt a pulse.

'She's not dead. Have you rung for an ambulance?' he called over his shoulder.

Edwina, who was standing in the hall in shocked silence, answered: 'No, but I've called for Doctor Trotter. He should be here any minute. He'll know what to do for the best. If he rings for an ambulance they'll come from Orange, but it'll take a while. Our station closed last year.'

Hodgkiss went out to the hall then to the front door and called out to the two shadowy figures hovering near the front gate. 'I think it would be as well if you stayed where you are. Miss Fink has been injured and the fewer feet we have tramping around the place the better.'

Pat called back. 'That sounds like the sort of thing Donald tells you when he's trying to keep you away from a crime scene.'

Hodgkiss smiled. 'Yes it does, doesn't it. But I really can't say if this is a crime scene or not but I'm not taking any chances. Edwina has called a doctor and Vera, you might call the hospital and get a message to Sergeant Flack and ask him to come here ASAP. Meanwhile I'll try to ascertain what happened.'

He turned to Edwina who had sat on the edge of an uncomfortable-looking wooden chair in the hall. 'Do you feel up to telling me what happened here? You don't have to, of course, and you might think it wise not to say anything until you have a solicitor present.'

'Oh, no there's no need for that,' Edwina said. 'I didn't do anything wrong except perhaps I was rather abrupt with her … even quite rude I suppose.'

'But your face …'

Again Edwina raised a hand to her cheek where Hodgkiss could now see long scratch marks.

'I'm afraid I made Miss Fink rather angry and she … well,

she went for me. You see she's never really approved of me, not since I had some of the trees in the school yard lopped because the children loved to climb them and they were always falling out and breaking arms and things. And I was afraid the gums might drop a limb on the children one day. And then there was poor Arthur tying up his little dog outside the cottage. She certainly didn't approve of us … me and Arthur.'

'And how did you come to be in the house here?'

Edwina continued. 'Well after you and your friends left to go to the hospital I began thinking about the typewriters missing from their boxes in the storeroom and I decided to confront Miss Fink about it … ask her if she'd taken them. You see I was rather upset at the thought of someone just walking in and taking what they wanted although I must say I couldn't see Miss Fink doing it on her own. And as it turned out she didn't. She had help.'

'Mrs Meadows, no doubt,' said Hodgkiss.

'Yes, of course. That's what I thought. Anyway I came across, knocked on her door and when she answered I said there were a few things I needed to speak to her about. And what do you think she did?'

'Shut the door in your face.'

'Yes, or she tried to. But I put my foot in the door and told her I wasn't going away until I found out what I wanted to know. So she said to come in and asked what was it that was so urgent that I had to break into her home.

'First off I asked her if she'd taken any typewriters from the school storeroom. She denied it of course. Then I mentioned the five little wooden things that her pot plants were standing on and told her that I knew what they were for and that she could only have got them by stealing them from the school.

'She denied it of course. She laughed at me.

'Then I just came straight out and accused her of stealing five typewriters and asked where she'd put them.

'She denied that she had any typewriters. So I decided not to waste any more time arguing with her and started looking around the house.

'She followed me around from room to room until we got to the little back bedroom next to the kitchen. When I tried to open the door to that room she pushed me away quite violently.

'Of course I knew at once that that was where she kept the typewriters. So I tried the door, but it was locked. Now I know that in most of these old places one key will usually unlock all the inside doors. So I went down the hall to the front room because I'd seen a key in the door there. I took the key out and went back down to the room where I thought the typewriters were.

'When I got there she was standing in front of the door with her arms crossed in front of her. She said to me: 'Take one step closer and I will kill you.

'Of course it wasn't very pleasant being threatened like that but I wasn't going to let her put me off. So I stepped forward, went to push her away and she lashed out at me … at my face.

'That made me mad and I took hold of her wrists in one hand and held them down while I unlocked the door. Once the door was open she seemed to quieten down.

'When I saw those typewriters … five of them sitting on tables in that room … I thought of all those wicked letters that she'd written and how she'd probably been the cause of Arthur taking his own life. I was really angry.

'She must have seen that because she turned and hurried back down to the front room.

'But I hadn't finished with her. I wanted to hear her confess to writing the letters …and to tell her what I thought of her.

'When I got to the front room she'd closed the door but couldn't lock it because that was the door where I'd taken the key out.

'I tried to open it but she was holding tight onto the handle and probably had her foot against the door as well because I couldn't budge it an inch. Of course that was before I'd really tried to use force to get in. I asked her to let me open the door because I hadn't finished speaking with her. But she wouldn't. She shouted out at me through the door calling me all sorts of horrid names. So I turned the handle sharply and started pushing the door. I had no idea how strong she was because I couldn't force it open … not at first.

'Then I put all my weight against it and shoved hard. That did the trick.

'But as the door flew open I heard her give a cry and saw her stagger back into the room and fall down, holding her head.

'I think the door must have hit her because there was blood running down the side of her neck.

'I was pretty shocked when I saw her like that. I went in to try to see if there was anything I could do to help. I tried to feel her wrist for a pulse but there didn't seem to be anything and I thought I must have killed her.

'I rang for the doctor straight away and phoned the police station. Then I went out on the front veranda and just sat there in a bit of a daze. I didn't see that there was anything more I could do. I know a bit of first aid but none of what I had learned seemed to apply to Miss Fink.

'Then you came … and your friends. I was very glad to see you Mr Hodgkiss.'

'And now I'd say that's Dr Trotter arriving now,' said Hodgkiss hurrying out to the front verandah.

*　　*　　*

Dr Trotter was a short, rotund man, energetic for his seventy years, most of them spent tending to the health of the people of Narrolong and district.

He hurried into the room, a large black bag clutched in one hand.

'Knock on the head, eh,' he commented as he knelt down. 'She's going to have a nasty headache in the morning.' He turned to where Hodgkiss and Edwina stood behind him. 'Was anyone with her at the time?'

Before Edwina could get a word out Hodgkiss said. 'Yes, this young lady was here. It was she who called you. She called for the ambulance too.'

'Did she?' said Dr Trotter absently, turning back Miss Fink's eyelids to examine the pupils. 'Well we're in luck there because the ambulance is here at the moment bringing one of my patients back from hospital. In fact I saw them parked near the police station. That's probably them how,' he said nodding his head towards the street. 'I'll have her taken to hospital and the staff there will keep her in for observation for a day or two then she should be able to come home. There's nothing wrong with her that a day or two of bed rest won't fix.'

He closed his bag and stood up.

'Hello, looks like she's waking up,' he said.

Miss Fink's eyes were open and she was making feeble efforts to rise.

'Stay where you are, Miss Fink,' the doctor said. 'You're going off to hospital for a day or two. You'll be better in no time. You've had a nasty whack on the head.'

Miss Fink started began to speak; 'Before I go, doctor …'

But Dr Trotter waved her to silence. 'Just you relax, Miss

Fink, Don't try to talk. Now here's the ambulance to take you to hospital. A day or two there and you'll be back to your old self in no time,' he said cheerily.

Suddenly the room was crowded as three burly men in ambulance uniform appeared, bringing with them a collapsible stretcher. Miss Fink was placed on the stretcher, restraining belts put in place and she was gone, Doctor Trotter hurrying in their wake.

Hodgkiss remarked. 'I don't think we want Miss Fink back here as her old self, do we, Edwina.'

But Edwina lowered her head. 'I feel terribly guilty about what happened. It was all my fault.'

'Nonsense,' Hodgkiss snapped. 'She brought it on herself. You were quite within your rights to come and demand an explanation. After all there can be no doubt it was she who wrote those appalling letters.'

'Yes, but it wasn't just her. Mrs Meadows was in it. She typed several of them.'

'Did she tell you that?' Hodgkiss asked, tossing his head in the direction of the street where the ambulance could be heard departing.

Edwina nodded. 'But I suppose she could deny it if it suits her later when they bring her home. I suppose Mrs Meadows wouldn't want everyone to know that she'd been in it too.'

They had just turned to leave the room when Edwina stopped and pointed. 'What's that ... on the floor.'

The two returned to the centre of the room and looked down.

On the floor boards was a mark drawn apparently in dark blood.

'I think I know what it is,' said Hodgkiss. He took the phone from his shirt pocket. 'I'll take a photo of it and email it to Vera. She'll know for certain.'

The phone flashed as he took the photo, then his fingers moved quickly over the keypad as he sent the email.

'So what is it d'you think? Edwina asked.

'I'm pretty sure it's a shorthand outline, but I've no idea what it says. Vera went to Miss White's secretarial college so she should be able to read it.'

'But what about Miss Fink. I never heard that she could write shorthand.'

'Oh yes,' said Hodgkiss. 'She knew how to write shorthand all right. In fact Miss White, who ran the school, told us Miss Fink was in the same class as Vera although she was never as good.'

Edwina shook her head. 'She must have been laying over it. Perhaps she became conscious after she collapsed and wrote it then while I was sitting outside waiting for the doctor to come. Perhaps her arm was across it. I wonder what it says.'

Moments later Hodgkiss phone sounded its ringtone. 'Well, we'll soon know.'

He read the screen and, smiling, turned it for Edwina to see.

He said. 'It would appear that Miss Fink experienced an epiphany of sorts during her trials.'

The message on the screen from Vera's phone read:

It's a shorthand outline all right. There is of course more than one word that can be read from this outline but by far the most likely is **accident**. *It could read* **occident** *but why on earth would she write that. Although there was no line under the outline to show the position of the word and thus its initial vowel, there's no doubt in my mind about what it reads because she put in the short* **a** *vowel on top of the* **k** *stroke. Hope this helps. Vera.*

'It most certainly *does* help,' said Hodgkiss.

'It most certainly helps me,' said Edwina. 'I was terrified that Sergeant Flack was going to take me away and charge me with murder. I wonder why she did it … bothered to write that.'

Hodgkiss said. 'Unlikely as it may seem I'd say Mis Fink suffered a serious attack of conscience.'

*   *   *

'I hear they've kept her in hospital. Looks like she might have been hurt worse than they thought.'

Sergeant Flack was sitting at Vera's kitchen table, a mug of black coffee in one hand.

Since Pat and Hodgkiss had announced their intention to return to Sydney that afternoon Vera had invited the sergeant and Edwina for brunch to farewell her visitors.

Hodgkiss asked. 'And has she made a statement about what happened after Edwina dropped over for a chat?' Hodgkiss asked.

The sergeant nodded. 'I haven't spoken to her yet but she made a statement to Constable Beasley at the hospital. Then she had a relapse. The nurses are worried about her. Thinking of transferring her now.'

'I suppose she confessed to writing all those awful letters, did she?' said Vera.

Sergeant Flack shook his head. 'No. Not on your life. From what Beasley's told me so far she reckoned that Martha Meadows wrote them. She said all she did was type up the envelopes and that she had no idea what Martha was putting in the letters.'

'But that's nonsense,' said Pat. 'She must have known what

was in them. There was gossip about them all around town. Everybody knew.'

'Yeah, I know,' said the sergeant. 'But Miss Fink claims that she thought that Marta was only writing about anti-tree lopping stuff. It's possible, I suppose. Anyway, I've sent all the typewriters off to forensic testing so they might be able to tell us which of them used which typewriters and which ones were used for the envelopes and which for the letters.'

'And what has Martha got to say about it? Does she admit to typing the things?' Pat asked.

'I haven't had a chance to talk to her yet. I'll do that today after I've had a chance to read all of Miss Fink's statement. They're going to email it through to the station. It's probably there by now.'

'So will anyone be charged, d'you think?' Vera asked.

'That's not up to me,' said the sergeant. 'I'll just take a statement from Mrs Meadows and see what comes of that.'

'I suppose someone … probably Martha … stole those typewriters from the school storeroom.'

'Yes, and according to Miss Fink that was Mrs Meadow's idea. She reckons she had nothing to do with it … that Martha just turned up with them one evening and those little wooden platform things she sat her pot plants on.'

Hodgkiss asked. 'And did she say anything that might give a clue to why she had the attack of conscience that led her to write *accident* on the floor in her own blood?'

Sergeant Flack shook his head. 'No. Not really. Beasley asked her about that but she was pretty out of it by then. I suppOse I'd better be getting on my way. Things to do.'

Sergeant Flack pushed back his chair and rose. Just then his phone sounded its ring tone. He took the phone from his jacket opened the connection and listened. His face grew grave.

He closed the connection. 'Poor old thing. She died during the night. Well at least she managed to tie up the loose ends for us before she went. Well, I'd better be getting back down to the station and have a look at that statement.'

Hodgkiss said. 'It won't be much use to you now, will it. Martha Meadows will say it's the ravings of a concussed old woman.'

Sergeant Flack nodded. 'Very likely. But deathbed statements *do* carry some weight.'

'Yes. If the person thought they were dying. Perhaps she wished she was already dead. She couldn't have faced the town once it came out that she typed the envelopes. If she typed them.'

Sgt Flack held out a hand to Hodgkiss. 'Nice meeting you, Edgar and you too, Pat. I hope I'll see you both again some time.'

Vera shook her head. 'It's not easy to lure Pat away from the comforts of the city. We might have to wait for out next crime wave before I'll be able to lure them both back here again.'

*   *   *

It was two in the afternoon when the goodbyes were finished and Pat backed the Mercedes carefully out of the driveway of Vera's home then down the hill towards the Narrolong township.

'I suppose Vera's right,' said Pat. 'It's pretty unlikely that we'll ever be back.'

Hodgkiss nodded. 'Most unlikely, I'd say. But it was an interesting little problem.'

'I wouldn't have called it interesting,' said Pat. 'A rather depressing business I'd've called it.'

'Oh yes, it was that all right. Dreadful people doing dreadful things to each other.'

They fell silent until they were about five minutes outside the town and the cemetery came into sight.

Hodgkiss reached over and touched Pat's arm. 'Isn't that Edwina standing there in the cemetery?'

'I believe you're right,' said Pat. 'No doubt saying goodbye to her boyfriend.'

'Would you mind stopping? There's one or two things I need to ask her.'

Pat slowed and pulled the big car onto the unmade shoulder. 'Do you want me to come with you?' she asked.

Hodgkiss thought before answering. 'I don't see why not.'

The two climbed out and made their way into the cemetery then between the gravestones to where Edwina stood beside a raw mound of red earth, head bowed.

She heard them and turned. 'No head stone as yet,' she said. 'I've paid for it. It would have taken forever if I waited for the executors to make the arrangements.'

'That's good of you,' Hodgkiss said softly.

'The very least I could do for the poor man.' She left a short silence.

Hodgkiss said softly. 'I suppose you've heard about …'

'Her dying. Yes. I'm so sorry in spite of what she did.' She paused. 'You're on your way home I suppose.'

Hodgkiss nodded but said nothing.

Edwina asked. 'I think you could say your investigation has been a success. At least that's what they're saying in town; that Vera's detective from the city solved the case.'

Hodgkiss smiled wanly. 'Is that what they're sayings is it. I wish it was true.'

Edwina looked at him surprised. 'You don't think so? You

don't think you solved it … the letters … who wrote them.'

'The letters …yes. But the letters were only one of the problems.

'The only one that matters now,' Edwina said. Then she asked: 'Have they finished all the forensic tests yet?'

'On the typewriters, you mean? I really don't know and I don't care. As I said, *that* problem is solved.'

'Then what else is there to know?' Edwina asked. Pat detected an edge of anxiety in the woman's voice.

Hodgkiss looked directly at Edwina. 'What else indeed.'

Pat heard an unmistakable threat in his tone. 'Time to go, Hodgkiss,' she said, turning and heading back to the car.

Hodgkiss said. 'Goodbye, Edwina,' and followed Pat.

Pat had not driven far when she asked, without turning her head. 'And what was all that about?'

'All what?' Hodgkiss said, prepared to be difficult.

'You as good as accused the girl of something?'

'Did I? Yes, I suppose I did.'

'Then what was it? What is it you think she did?'

'There were a couple of questions that I wanted answered, but in the end I thought it best not to know.'

'What questions? Or don't you want to tell me?'

'Oh I don't mind telling you. It was to do with that short-hand outline.'

'Don't you think it said *accident*. That it could have read something else.'

'Oh no. I've no doubt it was meant to say *accident*. I was interested that Edwina asked about the forensic tests, weren't you?'

'No. Not particularly. Why? What was so interesting about that? It was a reasonable enough question to ask.'

'Yes, it was. But she asked in particular if they had

finished *all* of the forensic tests, not just the tests on the five typewriters.'

'But what other forensic tests were there?'

'None. That's what Edwina wanted to know. I think she was concerned about the blood on the floor … the blood used to write the shorthand outline. She wanted to know if it had been tested too.'

Pat frowned. 'But why should they have tested that? It was Miss Fink's blood. Wasn't it?'

'Was it? I don't know. Miss Fink wasn't the only person there who was bleeding.'

Pat fell silent, concentrating through the windscreen.

Then. 'So you think that Edwina wrote it?'

'No … but she might have.'

'But she doesn't write shorthand, does she?'

'I've no idea. But if she never learned shorthand and somehow she *did* write that outline then there is a very nasty implication.'

'You mean she learned how to write the outline before she went across to see Miss Fink … that she went there intending to …'

Pat shook her head. 'No. I don't believe it, Hodgkiss. She's not that kind of person. Is she?'

'No. I agree. She isn't.'

They had been driving for only five minutes when Hodgkiss' phone rang. He took it from his shirt pocket and examined the screen.

The message was from Vera.

I didn't mention it before, but whoever wrote that outline on the floor was no expert. Anyone with the most basic knowledge would have written it in a much shorter form.

Hodgkiss turned off the phone and returned it to his pocket.

'And what was that about?' Pat asked with a sharp glance in Hodgkiss' direction.

Hodgkiss shook his head. 'Nothing. It was nothing.'

There was a longish silence in the car, then Pat said: 'We'll stop for afternoon tea at Mount Victoria.'